the
Trouble
with
May
Amelia

the Trouble with May Amelia

Jennifer L. Holm

ILLUSTRATED BY Adam Gustavson

ATHENEUM BOOKS FOR YOUNG READERS
NEW YORK LONDON TORONTO SYDNEY

ATHENEUM BOOKS FOR YOUNG READERS
An imprint of Simon & Schuster Children's Publishing Division
1230 Avenue of the Americas, New York, New York 10020
Text copyright © 2011 by Jennifer L. Holm
Illustrations copyright © 2011 by Adam Gustavson
Photograph on page 206 courtesy of the author.
For information about special discounts for bulk purchases, please contact Simon & Schuster Special Sales at 1-866-506-1949 or business@simonandschuster.com.
The Simon & Schuster Speakers Bureau can bring authors to your live event. For more information or to book an event, contact the Simon & Schuster Speakers Bureau at 1-866-248-3049 or visit our website at www.simonspeakers.com.
Book design by Sonia Chaghatzbanian
The text for this book is set in Goudy Old Style.
The illustrations for this book are rendered in pen and ink.
Manufactured in the United States of America
1210 FFG
10 9 8 7 6 5 4 3 2 1
CIP data for this book is available from the Library of Congress.
ISBN 978-1-4169-1373-3
ISBN 978-1-4424-2140-0 (eBook)

For Millie May
who is No Trouble at all
-J. H.

If nothing is dropped, nothing will be found.

—Finnish proverb

Contents

the
Trouble
with
May
Amelia

Ivan Alvin Wilbert Isaiah Wendell Kaarlo

Me.

CHAPTER ONE

Irritating as a Grain of Sand

My brother Wilbert tells me that I'm like the grain of sand in an oyster. Someday I will be a Pearl, but I will nag and irritate the poor oyster and everyone else up until then.

Wilbert has found me here on the Baby Island where I have to come to hide from Pappa who is Spitting Mad at me. I washed out the jar of yeast starter and we won't have bread for a week. Pappa says I'm Just Plain Stupid because I Never Pay Attention and that he would rather have one boy than a dozen May Amelias because Girls Are Useless. I don't know why he would want any more boys seeing as he already has seven.

These are my brothers:

Matti is nineteen and he ran away not that I blame him.

Kaarlo is eighteen and our cousin, although we think of him as a brother. We also think of him as cranky.

Isaiah is seventeen.

Wendell is sixteen.

Alvin and Ivan are twins and fifteen.

Wilbert is fourteen, and my Best Brother.

May Amelia Jackson is twelve. That is Me.

We live on the Nasel River in the state of Washington. It is 1900 and I Am in Trouble Again.

Wilbert is always telling me that I need to find my *sisu* or I will never make Pappa proud of me. *Sisu* is a Finn word that means to have guts and courage. I want to say that it is very hard indeed to have *sisu* when you're the only girl on the Nasel.

Come on out of there, May, Wilbert says. You got to stop running away.

But I am content where I am in the old sorcerer tree. It is a hollowed-out tree that fits a child like me just fine and is my secret spot. Not a soul knows about it except Wilbert and he is my Best

Brother and would never tell anyone, not even the nosy wind.

You can't stay in there forever, Wilbert says.

I can so, I say.

May, he says.

I ain't budging.

It's suppertime, he says.

Fine, I say and crawl out of the tree.

Out here in Washington there are no roads but we have the Nasel so we take rowboats everywhere. I learned to navigate when I was only five, although none of the boys let me steer except Wilbert.

The Nasel stretches out before us like a winding snake. On either side, the mountains rise green and thick. It's spring, and the sky is gray as the slates we use at school. It's only ever sunny in my dreams.

Uncle Aarno is sailing down the river in his mail boat, the *General Custer*. Uncle Aarno is a gillnetter and he is Pappa's brother. He looks just like Pappa, except that he smiles and has laughing eyes and a kind way about him.

Give that to your mother, he says, passing me a letter. Don't let your father see it.

I take the letter from him and ask, Thought up any new ways to die lately?

Uncle Aarno is always talking about How He's

Going To Meet His Maker. He keeps a list of ways he might die:

Drowned in the Nasel.
Swept out to sea in a storm.
Poisoned by a bad oyster.
Shanghaied to the Orient.
Bludgeoned in a back alley in Astoria.
Bored to death by the preacher in church.

Uncle Aarno nods and says, Eaten By A Cougar.

That's a good one, I say. Some mean cougar has been picking off our sheeps and if he keeps it up, we ain't gonna have any wool socks this winter.

Sounds like a job for Wild Cat Clark, Uncle Aarno says.

We best be going, Uncle Aarno, Wilbert says. We got to milk the cows and May Amelia can't get into any more trouble with Pappa or he'll disown her.

What did you do this time? my uncle asks me.

I was washing dishes and I washed out the yeast starter.

My brother does like his bread, Uncle Aarno says sympathetically.

It was An Accident! I say and Wilbert says, Poor May is the only person who can make An Accident out of washing the dishes.

Uncle Aarno chuckles and says, You better get going then.

Our farm is in the middle of nowhere and there is nothing but land and trees and cows and sheeps and bears and brothers. There are no other girls here to play with me. My baby sister Amy died over the winter and she is buried on the Smith Island along with a piece of my heart. Just thinking about her makes me sad, and then it starts to rain, misty-fuzzy rain that sticks in your hair and makes you feel clammy. It rains so much here that our poor horses have rain rot on their hides.

May Amelia! a voice cries.

It's Berle Holumbo coming down the Nasel after us in his boat. Berle's my age and has got a droopy eye, and is missing one of his front teeth from where he fell out of the hayloft. He sure ain't much to look at. He pulls his rowboat alongside ours.

Hi Berle, Wilbert says.

Hi Wilbert, Berle says and turns to me and smirks, Hiya May Amelia.

What do you want, Berle? I ask.

Eating a lot of bread lately? he asks with a smirk.

How'd you hear about it? I demand.

Isaiah told my ma what happened and she sent me along to give this to you, Berle says, holding out a jar of yeast starter.

I take it from him.

Ain't you gonna say thanks? Berle asks, scratching his neck.

Ei, I say, which means No in Finn.

As we row away, Berle hollers, Your sister ain't got no manners, Wilbert!

Least I ain't got lice! I shout back.

Our neighbor's boy, Lonny, is at the farm when we get home. He is wandering the yard looking nervous.

Hiya, May Amelia, Lonny says.

The front of his shirt is wriggling around. Bosie, our scruffy dog, is standing at Lonny's feet, barking at him.

What you got in your shirt, Lonny? I ask.

Shhh, he says. Then he reaches inside and pulls out a tiny mewling kitten. It's from our cat Buttons's new litter.

Isaiah said I could have him, he says. But don't tell no one.

Why you keeping him in your shirt? I ask.

To hide him from Daddy, of course.

Lonny's a bit soft in the head on account of an accident he had when he was little, but his thinking is straight on this. Mr. Petersen doesn't like cats one bit. I once saw him drown a whole sack of them in the Nasel.

What're you gonna do with him when you take him home? I say.

Keep him in the shed, Lonny says with a lopsided grin.

I sure hope Mr. Petersen doesn't plan on going into the shed, Wilbert says under his breath.

May Amelia Jackson! a voice growls, and I whirl around. Pappa is standing there looking cranky as an old bear wearing a scraggly tangle of a beard.

Where Have You Children Been? Have you been Getting Into Trouble Again, May Amelia?

May got a new yeast starter, Pappa! Wilbert says quickly.

Humph, Pappa says, his two brows frowning like angry caterpillars.

Lonny pipes up, I been here the whole time, Mr. Jackson!

I know you have, Lonny, Pappa says and then narrows his eyes. What's that in your shirt, boy?

Ain't nothing in here, Mr. Jackson, Lonny says, but then the button on Lonny's shirt pops and the little kitten tumbles out and falls to the ground.

Ruuuf! Bosie yips at the kitten and the kitten turns tail and runs off and Lonny hollers, You Leave My Kitten Alone Bosie! and chases after them both.

Pappa sighs and barks at me, Go Help Your Mother, and then stomps away.

Mamma is peeling potatoes with a small paring knife. Her hands are fast; she is always in motion. I have never seen my sweet Mamma sitting still. I think she even works in her sleep.

There's my best Helper, Mamma says. She does not abide Hinderers in her kitchen.

I saw Uncle Aarno, I say and pull out the stained letter from my pocket. He wanted me to give you this.

Her eyes widen when she sees the handwriting on the letter.

Matti! she gasps.

Everyone thought my handsome oldest brother, Matti, got shanghaied out to sea when it turned out he just ran off with a local girl which was a real disappointment to me. I think for sure being shanghaied would've been a lot more interesting than eloping.

Mamma stares at the letter.

Open it, Mamma, I say.

Her hand trembles. When she finishes reading, she smiles. Thank Heavens he's fine! He and Mary are living in San Francisco and he's got a job working on the docks.

Is he coming home?

Your Father, she says and she doesn't have to say another word. Pappa would never understand Matti marrying an Irish girl. Pappa still thinks Matti's off somewhere in the Orient.

Mamma takes the letter and sticks it on the back of the shelf in the cupboard, behind the blackberry jam that she keeps for special occasions. She's got tears in her eyes when she turns around.

Are you all right Mamma?

I just worry about Matti. Your firstborn always has a special place in your heart.

I was your seventh-born. Do I have a special place in your heart? I ask.

Of course, May Amelia.

Am I special enough not to wash dishes after supper?

She laughs. Nobody's that special, May Amelia.

I cup my hands and holler for my brothers. Wilbert-Wendell-Isaiah-Ivan-Alvin-Kaarlo suppertime!

Bosie's the first one to come running. He's a dumb dog but he's smarter than all my brothers put together. Alvin and Ivan come ambling up a minute later. They are as alike as can be and they are both stinky.

Been mucking out the cow stalls? I ask.

Ivan wipes an elbow across his nose. Don't worry, May Amelia, we saved some for you.

And then Alvin grabs me and rubs me up against his overalls and then passes me over to Ivan who smears some manure in my hair.

Stop it!

Isaiah comes walking up and says, What're you

doing to May Amelia, Ivan? Isaiah is my gentle brother and cannot bear any fussing or fighting. I don't know how he survives in this family since that's all the boys do.

Let me go! I yelp.

Wilbert walks over and says, Leave Her Be, Alvin.

Alvin lets me loose and I stagger back right into Wendell who pushes his glasses up and sniffs. You smell like a cow, May Amelia.

That's just her natural perfume, Alvin cackles.

Ivan guffaws, Cow Perfume!

Wilbert can't help himself and a small laugh escapes his throat and Wendell has himself a chuckle and soon they are all laughing at me, saying Cow Perfume! Cow Perfume!

I stomp off. I should just go and live with the cows. It would be easier than being with all these useless boys.

Supper is boiled potatoes, *lutefisk*, and Noise. When all the boys are in the house, they shout and wrestle and argue and there is hardly space for a body to think. Sometimes I would rather live in the barn just so it would be quieter.

Lonny and his father, Mr. Petersen, come for supper as they often do since Mrs. Petersen died. It's the only way poor Lonny gets a decent meal. Mr.

Petersen needs to find himself a wife but women are scarce here.

Since I am the girl, it is my job to help Mamma so I serve everyone. Not a single boy thanks me when I put the lutefisk on his plate and I know why. Lutefisk is fish preserved with lye, and a more terrible thing I have never tasted. It smells like a dead animal that's been left in the sun to rot and then dipped in soap and looks even worse. None of us children can bear to eat it.

How much pasture you think I oughta set aside to make hay? Mr. Petersen asks my father.

Pappa considers this for a moment and then says, I'd do the whole north pasture. That should set you up fine.

All the other farmers are always asking Pappa for his opinion on things. They say my pappa has *sisu* because he scared a big bear out of a hollowed-out stump with just a look and lived in it when he first came to the valley. I've always felt sorrier for the bear. Pappa is pretty scary in the morning.

I slip a big chunk of my lutefisk on the floor under the table for Bosie.

Delicious supper, Alma, Mr. Petersen says with a burp.

Poor Mr. Petersen must be half-starved if he thinks lutefisk is delicious.

You're too kind, Oren, Mamma says with a smile.

There's *riisipuuro* for dessert! I tell Mr. Petersen. *Riisipuro* is Finn rice pudding.

Wendell holds up his empty plate. Can I have my dessert now? he shouts. Wendell's ears went soft after an illness, and now he cannot hear unless he can see a person's lips.

Yeah, Kaarlo says, frowning at the lutefisk. Can we have dessert first?

Your mother worked hard to make this so Eat, Pappa growls, and everyone falls silent.

A fella came to see me, Mr. Petersen says. He told me some folks are putting together money to build a town and that the train will come to it.

A train? Here in Nasel? Kaarlo asks in a shocked voice.

Mr. Petersen leans back. The man said we've got a good harbor. They're looking for investors. They say we're perfectly situated. They've even got a name for the town all picked out—Stanley. Has a nice ring to it!

Pappa grunts. Don't have any money to invest. I just finished paying off the new barn.

You don't need money when you got land, Mr. Petersen explains. Just mortgage it. The fella swears we'll be rich.

Mamma puts her hand on Pappa's. Can't hurt to listen to what the man has to say, Jalmer.

I start to clear away the empty plates, and that's when I see the little piles of lutefisk under the table by all the boys' chairs. I guess Bosie's not such a dumb dog after all.

The boys look around excitedly.

Pappa, if we get rich, can we get rid of May Amelia and get a new girl? Ivan asks. One who can cook good?

And mend clothes, Alvin says.

And clean, Ivan says.

And knit socks, Alvin adds.

But I do all those things already! I say.

If we get rich, we can get a new girl on one condition, Pappa declares.

What's that, Pappa? Kaarlo asks.

He gives a slow smile and says, She's gotta not stink like a cow.

The boys hoot with laughter and Kaarlo pounds on the table.

Isaiah turns to me and says, I think you smell real good, May Amelia. But then I sure do like cows.

CHAPTER TWO

This Is Bitter Country

The schoolhouse is on the Smith Island, which is upriver from our house. We children must take the rowboat to get there, and Wilbert says that rowboats have a bad habit of tipping over when May Amelia Jackson is sitting in them.

Wilbert calls, Hurry Up May Amelia Or You'll Be Changing Diapers!

This is my Best Brother's way of teasing me because Pappa is always saying that the only thing I need to learn is How To Change Diapers.

When I get to the boat, Wendell and Wilbert are

already there with Lonny. The older boys must stay home and help Pappa on the farm. No more school for them.

It's damp and chill and mist hangs on the river like smoke from the chimney. It's thick as fresh cream and we can barely see ahead of the boat.

Ghost day, Lonny says.

A lot of the old-timer Finns claim that when they came over they brought their ghosts with them along with their luggage. Misty days bring them out. The boys say that the ghosts want to scare you and steal your soul.

Lonny, Wendell says, there's no such thing as ghosts.

My brother Wendell wants to be a doctor, so he doesn't hold to things he can't squeeze between his fingers.

Look! Lonny says, pointing. There's one right there!

I strain my eyes and see a boat with two white-haired figures appear out of the mist.

Those are mighty small ghosts, Wilbert says with a chuckle.

It ain't ghosts at all. It's the Bighill kids—Emil and Eli. Emil, who's rowing, is five, and Eli is two.

Hi, May Amelia! Emil calls. His hair is so blond it's white.

What're you doing?

He holds up a tin pail. Daddy forgot his lunch. You going to the schoolhouse?

Yep.

Be careful. Friendly got out again, Emil says.

Friendly is the most Unfriendly bull in the entire valley. He is a big, mean, ornery Jersey and belongs to Old Man Bakkila and is always escaping out of his pen and coming over to the schoolhouse to try and kill us children. He gored little Albert Oja's leg last year. Albert had to climb a tree to get away from him and it took three grown men to rope Friendly and drag him away.

Thanks, I say, and we start rowing again.

Mr. Bakkila should just put that animal down, Wilbert says.

A fierce wind comes up and the cap on Wendell's head goes flying off into the water.

My cap! he cries.

I'll get it, Wendell, I say leaning over the side of the boat.

Be Careful, May Amelia, Wilbert says.

The cap's floated out of reach, so I kneel on the edge of the rowboat and lean over.

I Got It! I say triumphantly, but then the boat gives a lurch.

As I tumble into the cold Nasel I hear Lonny say, There She Goes.

* * *

You Fell In Again?! Miss McEwing says when I walk into the schoolhouse, dripping wet.

But Miss McEwing, I say. I was trying to get Wendell's cap.

She just shakes her head and says, I swear you spend more time in the water than on the boat, child. Go on and get something dry from the Dunking Box before you catch a chill.

The Dunking Box is a box of old clothes that Miss McEwing keeps in a corner for times like these. They are all boys' clothes, of course, since there are all boys in the schoolhouse except for me, but that doesn't bother me on account of the fact that I wear overalls myself. My aunt Alice gave me a pretty new dress, but it's hard to climb a tree in a dress.

The little potbelly stove is burning so the schoolhouse is toasty, although it smells like the inside of a barn. Most of the children must do the milking before school in the morning, including us. If you close your eyes, you can almost hear the cows lowing along to Miss McEwing's lessons.

Good Morning, Children, Miss McEwing says loudly.

Good Morning, Miss McEwing, we say back.

Miss McEwing is the sweetest teacher we have ever had and she is also the prettiest one. Eligible bachelors from all over the valley are always showing up at the schoolhouse hoping for a chance with her. Wilbert says it will be a sad day when some man steals our teacher away, for married ladies are not permitted to teach.

The schoolhouse door opens and a little boy with blond hair in a bowl cut is shoved through. He tries to run back out but his mother shakes her head.

Sinä menet kouluun! she says in Finn which means, You Go To School!

The door shuts and the boy stands there with a belligerent look on his face. Poor Charles Hasalm hates going to the schoolhouse because he doesn't know a lick of English and refuses to learn.

Good morning, Charles, Miss McEwing says. We are so pleased you could join us today.

He just stands there like a cow stuck in the mud.

Please sit down, Charles, she says, and finally the boy goes and sits next to my brother Wendell and puts his head down on the desk and closes his eyes.

Miss McEwing sighs and says, Let's turn to our vocabulary lesson. Take out your slates, please.

Our schoolhouse is just bare wood floors and rough desks and benches. We children share double desks, but since I am the only girl, I have one all to myself. We are too poor to have pencils and tablets, so we use slates and chalk. Why we don't even have any real books except for the ones Miss McEwing brought with her and the only map on the wall is the one some child drew of the world. Nasel is the center and Finland is on the other side.

The first word is Bitter, our teacher says. Can anyone tell me what this word means?

My brother Wendell, who is the smartest child in the valley, raises his hand. He should just go to school for all of us.

It means Disagreeable, he says loudly.

Very good, Wendell, Miss McEwing says. Can anyone use Bitter in a sentence?

Berle sits in front of me and he is scratching his neck so hard that there is a red spot.

Wilbert raises his hand and Miss McEwing says, Go on.

Nasel is bitter country, Wilbert says.

Nuutti Nort waves his hand wildly and Miss McEwing nods at him.

Charles is bitter because he has to go to the schoolhouse! Nuutti says loudly.

I suppose I can't argue with that, Miss McEwing agrees. Anyone else?

I got one, Miss McEwing, Berle says.

Yes?

May Amelia is bitter because she smells like a cow, Berle pronounces, and grins back at me.

The rest of the children laugh.

I shoot my hand up and say, I got one, too, Miss McEwing!

Yes, May Amelia? Miss McEwing says.

Berle is bitter because he's got lice, I say.

I ain't got lice, Berle says, glaring at me.

Oh yeah? Then why're you scratching?

It's just fleas, he says.

Miss McEwing sighs again.

The lazy sun peeps from behind the clouds, and we children take our lunch pails outside. There are big stumps from where the men cleared the trees to make a spot for the schoolhouse. The stumps are wide as a child and we leap from one to the next, chasing each other around. Some of the boys are fishing because everyone knows that Miss McEwing is always especially sweet to the boy who catches her a fish for her supper.

After a while, nature has its way with me and so I go into the outhouse. The outhouse is uphill from an apple tree, and I can tell you that you'll never catch me eating any apples from that tree.

I'm sitting there doing my business when I feel the outhouse shudder. But before I can move, the outhouse tips over, with Me In It!

I scramble, tugging up my drawers, and push the door open. All the boys are standing around laughing.

Ha! Ha! Berle says, hooting with laughter. Now you really are a Bitter Girl!

That was a mean trick, Berle! I shout.

It was funny! he says, his droopy eye light with laughter.

What is going on out here! Miss McEwing exclaims. And What Happened To The Outhouse?

Must not have been steady, Berle says in an inno-cent voice. Why, it just plain tipped over!

Berle tipped me! I say.

Tip It Back Up, Berle, or I'll be having a word with your father, Miss McEwing says sternly.

The boys get the outhouse righted and then Miss McEwing claps her hands and says, Recess Is Over.

Everyone files into the classroom and takes their seat and Miss McEwing looks around and says in an exasperated voice, And would somebody please fetch Charles?

I go back out and peek under the schoolhouse, where Charles is curled up on the ground, staring out.

You gotta come in now, I say.

He frowns and says, Darn. I thought she forgot about me.

Miss McEwing is at her desk helping the younger children with their letters and we older kids are peeking out the window at a tall man with bright blond hair standing nervously outside the schoolhouse. His hair is slicked back real neatly and he's holding a bouquet of flowers that he must have picked along the way.

Who is it? I ask.

Looks like Ike Peldo, Waino Saargard says.

He's shaved, Wilbert says, shaking his head.

And combed his hair! Albert Oja says.

And that shirt looks pretty clean to me, Wendell adds with a frown.

Who's going? Nuutti asks, and they all look at me.

Fine, I say. I'll do it.

I go up to Miss McEwing carrying the tin water bucket and dipper and say, There's no drinking water.

Oh, dear, she says. I must have forgotten to fill it this morning. Would you be a dear girl and fetch some?

Yes, ma'am, I say.

I take the bucket and fill it from the barrel that catches rainwater next to the schoolhouse. When I'm done, I walk over to Ike Peldo. All the boys are watching me through the window.

You here for Miss McEwing? I ask him.

Uh, yes I am, the man says, his cheeks blushing red. I was hoping to speak with her after school is finished.

Are those flowers for her? I ask.

Picked them myself.

Oskari Talso gave Miss McEwing a real gold bracelet.

A gold bracelet! Ike gasps.

I nod. And Aaprami Suomela gave her a velvet hat. You should see it.

He bites his lip.

I lower my voice. I don't want to spoil the surprise, but Wild Cat Clark told me he's planning on getting her a cougar-skin cape.

A cape, he echoes.

But those sure are pretty flowers, I say.

Poor Ike looks down at his flowers and then hands them to me.

You can have them, he says. Then he slinks off, his shoulders lowered, and the boys cheer behind me.

I feel a little bad for the poor man, but I'd feel a whole lot worse for us if we lost Miss McEwing.

After school, I stay behind at the schoolhouse to help Miss McEwing clean. We shake down the cobwebs, and empty the ashes from the stove, and sweep the floors clear of mud clopped in by the boys. I don't mind cleaning here because Miss McEwing is interesting. She's been to faraway places like Pennsylvania and New Jersey and they sound thrilling, not like Nasel.

Why'd you come way out here? I ask her.

For a little excitement, I suppose, she says.

You must be real disappointed, I say. 'Cause there's nothing exciting here.

Well, my parents aren't very happy with me, she says.

Why? I ask. Did you wash out the yeast starter, too?

She gives me a funny look and says, Mother wanted me to marry and settle down.

Do you want to get married? I ask her.

She nods her head firmly. I very much do want to be married, May Amelia. I'm just waiting for the perfect man.

What's a Perfect Man?

She looks out the window. Oh, he has to have a kind heart and nice manners. And he has to love books, of course.

I don't know about that, I tell her. But if you want a fella who is smelly and spits and ain't much of a talker, I know quite a few.

We are doing our sums when little Charles runs into the schoolhouse and slams the door shut. He stands in front of it, his hands holding it closed.

Why, Charles, Miss McEwing says with a smile. I believe this is the first time you've ever come into the schoolhouse under your own steam.

24

Charles shouts in Finn, Friendly's After Me!

Albert topples right off his chair in a dead faint.

My goodness, Albert! Miss McEwing exclaims.

Did he get you? Berle asks.

Almost, Charles says.

What's Charles saying? Miss McEwing demands. What's going on?

Poor Miss McEwing is just as bad at speaking Finn as we are at speaking the English.

I say in English, Charles says Friendly's After Him!

That bull's out again? she says, and runs to the window. Every child leaps up from his desk and runs after her and peers out. Sure enough, Friendly's stomping and snorting around our schoolhouse.

You got a gun, Miss McEwing? Wilbert asks.

Our sweet teacher goes pale and says, All you children stay inside, you hear me? Now get back to your desks. There will be no recess outside today.

Thanks to Friendly we are all Very Bitter Children.

I haven't forgotten the mean trick Berle played on me. He thinks I'm just a dumb girl, but I know a thing or two because I've lived with a herd of boys my whole life.

The next day Friendly is nowhere in sight, so we children are allowed to play outside. Some of the boys have their fishing lines set in the Nasel, and Berle is one of them.

I creep up behind him and shout in Berle's ear, Watch Out Here Comes Friendly!

He's so startled he just falls right into the water!

When he comes up he's soaking wet and the school bell's ringing because recess is over.

Berle comes into the schoolhouse looking like a wet rat and glowering at me.

How'd you fall in? Miss McEwing asks.

May Amelia scared me! he says.

He tipped right over just like the outhouse! I say in my own defense.

Miss McEwing shakes her head and says, Berle, fetch yourself some dry clothes before you catch a chill.

Berle grabs the clothes out of the Dunking Box and stomps outside to the outhouse to change.

Miss McEwing begins reading from the McGuffey Reader to us. After a moment, she looks up and says, What is taking Berle so long?

I ain't coming in! Berle shouts from outside the schoolhouse door.

Why? she asks.

I just ain't!

Come in this instant! Miss McEwing says firmly.

The door bangs opens and Berle's standing there

wearing a dress. It's tight on him and has got puffy sleeves and a lace collar.

Ha! Ha! The children laugh. Berle Looks Like A Girl! Berle Looks Like A Girl!

Miss McEwing's eyes widen and she says, Why are you wearing a dress, Berle?

Because it was the only thing in the box, he says with a scowl.

Oh My, our teacher says, and puts her hand over her mouth to hide her amusement.

Wilbert looks at me. That your new dress? The one Auntie Alice gave you?

It sure looks a lot better on Berle, I say, laughing. The lace collar suits him fine.

CHAPTER THREE

No Kind of a Cook

Our chickens lay eggs and our cows make milk, but none of our animals can print money, so Pappa must go to work at the logging camp so that we can buy sugar and shoes. I am wearing a pair of handed-down shoes that Pappa has put new soles on three times. When I take them off at night, my feet stink of mud and manure and all the boys who wore them before me.

Pappa working at the camp breaks Mamma's heart, for it is the most dangerous place a body can work. The men call the trees that fall on them Widow Makers and if Pappa is even a few moments late for supper,

Mamma is at the window measuring a box in her head. Four blasts from the whistle at the logging camp means the death of someone's father or brother or son. Last year Mr. Korhonen was killed when a tree fell on him, and every mother in the valley was waiting at the bottom of the camp certain it was her man who had died.

I am helping Mamma with the chores. It is Monday, which is laundry day, and we are washing the sheets.

When we get to my room, there is Buttons curled up in the quilt on our bed surrounded by her kittens. Buttons loves sleeping with Wilbert and me. The kittens climb over each other, mewling away. They're greedy little balls of fur, trying to get at their Mamma's milk.

May Amelia, put that cat and those kittens in the barn, or she will be floating down the Nasel by suppertime, Mamma says.

But she doesn't do any harm, I say.

But her fleas do, Mamma snaps.

It takes all morning to boil the laundry and hang it on the line. It is a thankless chore because I have never met a boy who cares if he sleeps in clean sheets. But there is one chore that is never finished and that is catching babies.

Aksel Nort comes tearing into our kitchen.

You got to come quick, Miz Jackson! the boy cries, panting. The baby's coming fast!

No baby ever comes fast, Mamma says.

Mamma is a midwife and she walks miles to catch a baby. She gets paid in pork or spuds, although Pappa never stops saying she should ask for real money. My mother always says that the sweetest sound in the world is a baby's borning cry.

She calmly picks up her birthing basket, where she keeps her sharpest needles and best silk thread.

Now May Amelia, she chides, Make Sure Supper Is Ready when your daddy gets home from the logging camp.

Oh No! Ivan groans, May Amelia's cooking supper.

We're gonna starve to death! Alvin moans.

The last time Mamma went to catch a baby and I had to cook supper, I roasted a chicken and made potatoes. But it took so long to catch the bird and chop its head off and pluck the feathers that it was in the oven for but a few minutes when Pappa came home and I had to put it on the table. When I cut into it, it was raw as a baby's bottom and the potatoes weren't done either, so we had no supper that night and Pappa said that I was No Kind of a Cook and that I would never get a husband and he would be stuck with me till the end of his days.

Yes, Mamma, I promise. And don't forget to fire a shot!

I won't, she assures me.

To announce what kind of babe has come into the world, Mamma will shoot a gun—two shots for a boy, and one for a girl. Truth is, she hardly ever fires one shot. Folks say that there's something in the Nasel water that breeds boys. And I should know, because I was the only girl around here until my baby sister Amy was born. We only had her for a short time before she got called back to Heaven, where I hope and pray there is sunshine every day.

Maybe it will be a girl, I say.

Maybe, she answers with a sad smile.

Everyone knows that boys get cranky when they are hungry, and Pappa is the biggest boy of all. I start making dinner right away so it is sure to be ready when he returns home.

I decide to make *laksloda*, which is salmon baked with milk and potatoes. I put all the fixings for the *laksloda* together and soon it is bubbling away and the whole house is filled with a wondrous smell. I can almost imagine the smile on Pappa's face when he walks in. He'll say, May Amelia, that is A Tasty Meal you have prepared.

Isaiah sticks his head through the kitchen door and he looks frantic.

Something got to the new calf! Round up the boys!

I race around the farm calling for my brothers,

but by the time we get to the north field, it's plain as my face that there's nothing to be done for the calf. What's left of it, that is.

Kaarlo pronounces judgment like a preacher.

Cougar, he says.

We got to do something! Isaiah pleads.

Wilbert says, Get Wild Cat Clark.

Wild Cat Clark is the best cougar hunter in the valley. Every boy dreams of being him because a dead cougar means fifty dollars in your pocket.

My cocky brother Ivan says, I'm a better shot than Wild Cat Clark.

Nobody's a better shot than Wild Cat Clark! I say, and Alvin the loyal twin says, Who asked you anyway?

Wendell is squinting back at the house.

Is That Smoke? he asks. Or are my glasses dirty?

I follow where he is looking and sure enough smoke is curling out the open window of the kitchen.

The *laksloda*! I cry.

We race back to the house and into the kitchen and when I open the stove my beautiful *laksloda* is all burned up, the milk dried out and of course Pappa walks in the door at that very moment.

That supper? he growls.

I bite my lip.

Well, Wilbert says, at least it's Done this time.

• • •

There's a knock at the door, and Jacob Clayton our neighbor is standing there holding a pie. Mr. Clayton is a good neighbor. When our roof broke he came over and worked all week to help us fix it.

I saw your mother leave, he says to me.

She's off catching a baby.

I figured as much, he says. I made a pie. You have your supper yet?

May Amelia burned it! Ivan says.

She's No Kind Of A Cook! Alvin adds.

Now that's no way for a gentleman to speak about a young lady, Mr. Clayton says to Alvin.

Ivan snorts and Alvin says, May Amelia ain't no lady!

We eat Mr. Clayton's delicious mincemeat pie for supper and drink it down with fresh milk from our cows. After our bellies are full, we sit by the fire and the boys polish their guns and the men smoke their pipes. Mr. Clayton looks at the lumps of lead on the mantel.

Finns melt lead on New Year's to predict what will happen in the year to come. You pour the melted lead into water and you're supposed to be able to tell the future from the lumps. A ring or a heart means love, and a ship means travel, and if it looks like a pig, it means you won't go hungry. Last

33

New Year's we melted lead, and Pappa's lump was curved like a Boat, and Mamma's was a Ring, and my lump looked like an Ear. Pappa says mine meant that maybe I would finally learn to Pay Attention.

This one looks kind of like an Ear, Mr. Clayton says.

That's May's lump, Wilbert says.

I should've gotten an ear, Wendell says loudly.

Mr. Clayton asks Pappa, How is it up at the logging camp?

Pappa grunts. Lars the Swede will make them rich yet, the way he drives the crew.

Where'd you learn to make pie? I ask Mr. Clayton.

A surgeon taught me, he says, flexing his hand. Mr. Clayton's from the south originally and had three of his fingers shot off in a battle.

A surgeon? Wendell asks.

During the war, I worked in the tents where they brought the wounded and most of them weren't nothing but boys and all they wanted was their mammas. Since we couldn't give them that, one of the surgeons told me that pie was the next best thing. It would remind them of home.

How come the surgeon didn't sew your fingers back on? I ask.

Because we couldn't find them after they got blown off, Mr. Clayton says.

Did you look real good? I ask him.

Believe me, he says, I looked.

A clear shot rings through the night air.

It's a girl! I say.

Pappa puffs on his pipe, and says, Bad luck for them.

We spend the afternoon putting in the spuds. Mamma wants to get them in early so that she can sell them to the logging camp before everyone else. Mamma is very clever like that.

Now it is suppertime and Mamma is pacing in front of the window. Pappa is late.

Where can he be? Mamma asks, but no one answers her.

The whistle starts blowing in the distance and everyone goes still and counts. One. Two. Three. Four.

Mamma turns so pale I think she's going to fall over.

Go! she says to me and Wilbert. Dear Heavens Go Now!

Get the drums, May! Wilbert orders me.

Wilbert and I run out of the house on the trail leading to Armstrong's logging camp. The forest is so thick that I must look straight up at the sky if I wish to see the light. We bang on drums made from tin cans as we walk through the trees so that the big black bears will be scared away and not eat us.

We reach the Weilen place. Old Man Weilen's setting on his front porch with his wife, Jane, who is a Chinook lady and our dear friend.

Whose boy are you? Old Man Weilen asks.

I ain't a boy! I'm May Amelia Jackson!

Jalmer Jackson's got nothing but boys, the old man insists.

That's May Amelia, Jane tells her husband. She pats his hand and says to us in a low voice, He gets a little confused sometimes.

Do you know who got hurt? Wilbert asks.

She looks sympathetic. No, she says. But I heard the whistles, and it's never good news.

As we run away I hear Old Man Weilen say, I tell you, that's a boy.

Men are racing around when we reach the logging camp. Uncle Niihlo is the first one I see. He is the husband of Mamma's sister Ana, who is still back in Finland. He is tall as the trees and one of the best loggers in the valley.

Who got hurt? Wilbert asks.

No one, Uncle Niihlo says.

But the four whistles? I say.

Uncle Niihlo frowns in annoyance and says, The new whistle punk can't count. We've had three wives up here already looking for their husbands' dead bodies.

They should hire me on, Wilbert says. I can count!

So Pappa's all right then? I ask.

He's fine, but he won't be home for supper. Old Lars wants us to work late so he can release the splash dam tomorrow.

The splash dam is a Marvel. They dam the river high up and gang all the logs behind it. When they release the dam, the force of all that water shoots the logs down the river to the boom and then they are rafted to the sawmill. The splash dam is also Dangerous. That's how Lonny got hurt. He was playing in the river when they released the logs and got banged up good and was never the same after that. Since then, they always send a boy to let folks know when the splash dam is going to be released so that no one's taking a bath or doing their washing when half the trees on the mountain come hurtling down.

Off in the distance I see a bushy beard.

There's Pappa! I say, and start running through the woods. I've nearly reached him when someone grabs me about the waist and wrenches me back and we fall on the ground. A huge tree comes crashing down right in front of me and one of the branches scrapes my leg.

That was close! Uncle Niihlo, my rescuer, hisses in my ear, and then everyone rushes over at once.

Pappa hollers at me.

You Foolish Girl You Almost Got Killed! Didn't You See That Tree Falling?

I didn't see it, Pappa, I say, and wince in pain.

You okay, May? Wilbert asks.

My leg hurts bad, I whisper.

Pappa peels back my torn overalls and shakes his head. There are slivers of wood beneath my skin and it's all bloody and raw.

Oh, Girl, he says on a sigh. Then he lifts me up gently and carries me to the cook, an old fella named Mr. Henrickson who's been at the camp forever and is also their makeshift doctor.

Pappa holds my hand while Mr. Henrickson tries to dig out the slivers, but it's no good. They're too deep. He slices off a piece of salt pork and puts it on my leg and bandages it with some strips of muslin.

Leave it on overnight, he instructs. Your mother will be able to dig those slivers out in the morning.

Can you walk? Pappa asks me.

I give a shaky nod.

Pappa orders, Wilbert take your sister home now. And May Amelia, Try Not To Get Yourself Killed!

❋　　❋　　❋

It's gone dark, the only light is from the twinkly stars and we can barely see them through the thick trees. My leg is throbbing now, and it's a long walk home.

You gonna make it? Wilbert asks, as I lean into him.

I grit my teeth and nod grimly.

Look, we're at Spiderweb Alley, he says. Not too far now.

The children call this part of the woods Spiderweb Alley because it's all fir trees, and there are spiderwebs everywhere.

Ugh! I say as a sticky lacy spiderweb clings to my face. Then I feel something crawling on the back of my neck and smack around.

Wilbert, I got a spider on me! Get it off!

It's just a little spider, May. You gotta get some *sisu*.

Why is everyone always telling me I need to get some *sisu*? Just living with a herd of brothers takes a whole lot of *sisu* if you ask me.

There's a rustling ahead of us and I shove Wilbert forward.

Walk in front of me, Wilbert, I say.

Why? he asks.

Because if a bear attacks us, he'll eat You first.

You'd miss me if I got ate, he says, laughing.

I'd still have six other brothers left, I say. That's plenty.

But you wouldn't have a Best Brother, he says.

And then I Hear It—a soft footstep behind us.

You hear that? I whisper, looking back into the dark. The shadows shake in the trees.

Hear what?

That noise, I say, and he shakes his head.

On second thought, maybe you should walk behind me, I suggest.

We keep on walking in the dark, or limping, and I hear it again, and it's closer this time. But when I look behind me I can't see anything but the darkness swirling.

Something's following us, I whisper.

Probably just a rabbit, Wilbert says.

I hear a crunch again, and that's it for me. I say Come On Wilbert, and he says It's Probably Just A Rabbit, and I say Fine Then I'll Let the Rabbit Eat You, and I take off fast as my aching leg will carry me through the woods—over fallen trees, and mossy ferns—and soon I can hear the sounds of Wilbert pounding behind me, and he's calling Wait For Me but I'm not stopping for a brother who don't listen to me, even if it is my Best Brother.

When I reach the front door of our house I fling it open, falling inside on the floor, and then Wilbert is tumbling in after me, slamming the door shut and trying to catch his breath.

You look like you've seen a ghost, May Amelia, Isaiah says.

Something was following us! I pant.

It was just a rabbit, Wilbert insists.

Wendell is peering out the window and he says in a soft voice, Never seen a rabbit with teeth that big.

All the boys rush over to the window and look out.

A Big Ole Cougar is pacing back and forth outside the door, sniffing like it's found its supper!

Ivan snatches up his gun, and shouts, Alvin! and Alvin opens the window and *blam!* There is a dead cougar lying in front of our house.

Ivan and Alvin grin at each other.

Fifty dollars! they say in unison.

Wilbert turns to me and says, You may be no kind of cook, May Amelia, but you surely would have made A Tasty Meal for that cougar.

You'd miss me if I got ate, I say.

I'd still have six brothers left, Wilbert teases.

But you wouldn't have a May Amelia, I say.

CHAPTER FOUR

We Live in Misery

It is the custom in Finland for people to take their last name after where they farm so there are a whole lot of folks walking around named Maki which means Hill. Even though we are the Jacksons, my brother Kaarlo thinks we should change our name to the Miserables because he says This Farm is Nothing But Misery and I hafta agree with him.

I'm standing in stinky marsh up to my knees try-ing to get one of our cows out of the mud. The Nasel has flooded the best part of our grazing land, turn-ing it thick as molasses. Pappa says the Nasel is like a fickle woman who can't decide which way she wants to go.

This cow's name is Patience. Mamma named her after Pappa's mother who wasn't very patient at all. Patience has been stuck here all morning and if we do not get her out she is going to die when the tide comes in. We got a rope around Patience's neck and Isaiah and Wilbert are tugging while me and Kaarlo are pushing from behind. But the cow won't budge.

Should've named her Stubborn, Kaarlo says.

Pappa's gonna skin us alive if we don't get her out, Wilbert mutters.

The cow flicks her tail in Kaarlo's face.

You Dumb Cow, he shouts in frustration. And then he mutters, I wish I'd been shanghaied.

More than anything, Kaarlo wants to make his own way in the wide world. But with Matti gone, there's even more work on the farm, and most of it falls to poor Kaarlo. Pappa will never let him leave now.

You should talk nice to her, Isaiah suggests. Isaiah's got a soft heart and loves all animals, even cows, who don't have any sense.

Talk nice to the cow? Kaarlo snorts.

Maybe Isaiah's right, I say. Who'd want to listen to your hollering?

Kaarlo's eyes darken.

The only thing this cow's gonna listen to is a

switch, he snaps, raising the leather switch. Out of my way, girl!

I try to move but my foot is stuck fast in the thick mud and I know how the cow feels. Kaarlo, I say but he's already bringing the switch down—

Right on *my* backside!

I screech so loud that they probably hear me clear across the river in Astoria!

Ow!!!

The cow bolts straight out of the mud.

I hate you, Kaarlo! I wail, rubbing my backside.

Kaarlo roars with laughter.

That's one way to get a cow out of the mud, Kaarlo says with a grin.

The smile on Kaarlo's face disappears the next morning when he finds out that Ivan and Alvin have taken jobs up at the logging camp. He and Pappa have a terrible fight.

I'm the oldest! Why can't I go? Kaarlo demands.

Because you are My Right Hand, Pappa says. I need you here on the farm. Now I don't want to hear another word.

Mamma leaves to catch a baby, and Pappa and Alvin and Ivan are all at the logging camp. The rest of us unlucky Jackson children are clearing stumps. Pappa has cleared the trees, but the stumps remain behind so that it looks like we are growing a crop of stumps. We used to dig them out by hand but now we use dynamite. It has taken us most of the morning to haul away one stump after Kaarlo blew it up.

Do we have to do that other stump, too? Wilbert asks, and Kaarlo says, If we don't I'll never hear the end of it from Pappa.

Kaarlo is the only one who is allowed to set the dynamite because it is so dangerous. It's easy to get blown up and I think even Uncle Aarno would agree that that would be a bad way to go.

It's ready, Kaarlo says. Everyone get back.

He lights the dynamite and we all run for shelter but coming up over the way is Wendell.

Wendell! I holler, but it's no use because he's deaf and the dynamite explodes and chunks of wood from the stump go flying in all directions like feathers flying off a chicken. When the dust settles, we rush over to where Wendell was standing. He's lying on the ground.

Is he dead? I ask, but he groans.

Kaarlo rolls him over. His glasses are broken but he's fine.

He opens his eyes and blinks.

Wonderful, he says. Now I'm Deaf and Blind.

Sunday is a day of rest but nobody bothered to tell the big bear who knocked down the fence in our field where our sheeps graze. We children must go straight home after church and start mending fences while Mamma and Pappa go visiting at Jacob Clayton's place.

Isaiah is talking softly to one of the sheeps.

How are you feeling today, Mr. Weilen? he asks. Isaiah names our sheeps after the neighbors.

Ivan and Alvin are going on about how Exciting it is to work at the logging camp.

Uncle Niihlo says I'm a natural, Ivan boasts.

Kaarlo stares stonily at the ground and I feel sorry for him. It's not fair.

You should see the stump Kaarlo blew up yesterday! I tell Ivan.

Nearly took off my head, Wendell says.

Wilbert says, May, are you cooking?

Why? I ask.

He points at the smoke leading to the sky over the ridge by our house.

No, I whisper and we all start running like mad, like crazy, to get to the house. Halfway there, we see Pappa and Mr. Clayton running in the same direction. They must have seen it, too, and Pappa shouts, Did You Burn Something Again, Girl? but I just shake my head.

The Barn! Kaarlo shouts.

Our barn is on fire, and the flames are licking at the sky like greedy fingers trying to catch a cloud.

Pappa is yelling at the boys to save our animals. He kicks the door open and a horse comes running out, its tail a burnt singe.

Buttons! I cry, and start to run for the barn but Wilbert holds me back and says, Don't Be Stupid, May, It's Just A Cat!

Soon rowboats start arriving with neighbors to see if we need help, but there's nothing to help as there's no stopping a barn fire. It's the worst kind of fire ever, and we're just lucky Pappa built it far enough away from the house or else we would be as homeless as our horses.

I sit on a log and watch it burn.

Berle Holumbo comes huffing up to me carrying a string of fish.

May! he shouts. I was fishing and saw the smoke! Anybody hurt?

My cat, Buttons, and her kittens are in there, I say, and feel the tears run down my cheeks.

Oh, he says awkwardly. Sorry to hear that.

But I just cry.

Berle looks a little desperate as he holds up his string of fish.

Look! I caught five, he says. You want 'em?

I stop crying, and hiccup.

What am I supposed to do with them?

I don't know, he says with a helpless shrug. Maybe

we can put 'em on some sticks and roast them by
your barn?

My mouth drops open.

And I'll get some spuds, he adds. Fish is always
good with spuds.

I feel a little smile coming on.

Can you whip up some dessert? I ask him.

Sure, he says, and grins. Looks like your barn is all
warmed up now. Perfect temperature for baking a pie.

I start laughing.

Pappa's face is gray as the morning sky.

This is terrible, Mamma says, her voice hoarse.
And we just finished paying it off!

We'll get through it, he says tiredly. Jacob says we
can put our hay in his barn come harvest.

Mamma puts her hands over her face.

This farm never gets easier, she whispers.

I'm walking out of the henhouse with a basket full of
fresh eggs when I see the man wandering around. It's
easy to tell he's not from around here because he's
short, and he's wearing a proper suit. The men in
these parts are tall as trees and they don't wear suits,
even when they get buried because it would be too
much of a waste. Pappa only has one decent Sunday
shirt.

Hello there young fella, he says to me.

I ain't no boy! I say.

The man chuckles and twists his mustache in amusement.

Well, I'll be darned. The overalls had me fooled, young lady. Is your daddy at home?

I sit the man down in the parlor and fetch Pappa.

Pappa, I say. There's a fella to see you in the parlor.

The man stands up when Pappa walks in and he holds a card out and says, Your neighbor 'cross the way suggested I talk to you. Pleased to meet you. I'm F. B. Yerrington.

Pleased meet, Pappa says slowly, his tongue tripping over words like they are roots in the ground. Pappa never got the hang of speaking English.

When I start to walk out of the room, Pappa calls to me and says, in Finnish, Stay.

Yes, Pappa?

I need someone to translate for me, he says gruffly, and I know he is embarrassed.

Pappa hates that he does not understand what folks are saying to him, especially after he got swindled when he sold a cow. He likes one of us children to be with him when he has to speak English. It used to be my older brother Matti but he left so now it's Wendell. None of the other boys speak English any good at all.

I'll go fetch Wendell, I say.

I want you, he says.

Me? I say, surprised.

Wendell's deaf as can be and I want to hear right what this fella has to say. He's that man Mr. Petersen was talking about. You translate every word he says, you understand me?

Yes, Pappa, I say, and my heart swells with pride that he thinks I'm as good as a boy.

My girl speak for me, Pappa says in rough English to the man.

Why, of course, Mr. Yerrington says, and smiles at me. And what a lovely girl she is!

I translate that for Pappa and he says to me in Finn, Either He's a Liar, or You Can't Translate.

Mr. Yerrington starts talking.

As you may have heard, he says, I represent the interests of a group of gentlemen who are looking to develop this part of the country. We believe it is the perfect place for a new town. You have deep water for a port, ready access to timber, and an easy shipping route. We believe this will be the next Seattle, and we are looking for other like-minded men to join us in our venture.

I translate for Pappa as quickly as I can, but I stumble over some of the words and wish that I had paid better attention in the schoolhouse.

Mr. Yerrington pulls out a brochure and hands it to Pappa. It's printed in English.

FACTS, NOT FANCIES
CONCERNING THE FUTURE
GREAT SEA-PORT
and
COMING CITY OF THE PACIFIC COAST:
STANLEY!
AND THE MAGNIFICENT NASEL HARBOR!

I have some very influential supporters, Mr. Yerrington says. A United States senator is putting up considerable funds and we are anxious to move forward. We even have connections to get the railroad put through here. *Powerful connections*, he adds for emphasis.

How does it work? Pappa asks.

Should you invest with us, you will become a major stockholder in the Stanley Company. It is our intention to develop the land and sell lots to eager homeowners from back East. Once the majority of the lots have been sold, you will be free to cash in your stock and enjoy your newfound wealth.

Pappa looks uncertain.

Your neighbor, Mr. Petersen, has already agreed to invest, Mr. Yerrington says.

Ask him about Jacob, Pappa orders.

Is Mr. Clayton gonna be part of it? I ask.

It certainly looks that way, Mr. Yerrington says.

Yes, I tell Pappa.

How much are these stocks gonna be worth? Pappa asks.

Mr. Yerrington nods sagely. I can give you a conservative estimate only. Based on previous experience, we would say that your share of the stock will be worth a quarter of a million dollars.

I turn to Pappa and say, A quarter of a million dollars!

The stony look on Pappa's face never changes, but his eyebrow twitches and I know he's as shaken by the words as I am.

Opportunities such as this come only once in a lifetime, Mr. Yerrington says, smoothing his mustache.

I'll think on it, Pappa says.

Late that night, Mamma and Pappa sit talking at the table. I hide by the kitchen door, spying in.

We'd have to take a mortgage out on the farm, he tells Mamma.

It sounds like a good opportunity, Mamma replies.

Oren and Jacob are investing, Pappa says. Jacob isn't foolish.

Jacob is a wise man, Mamma agrees quickly.

Wouldn't have to worry about money ever again, Alma, Pappa says, his eyes gleaming.

Build a new barn, Mamma says.

I sneak back upstairs to the bedroom I share with Wilbert. He's already asleep and he's stolen all the covers as usual. I would give anything to have my own bed. I shake him awake.

You think Pappa will invest? I whisper to Wilbert.

I don't know, he says sleepily, and I look out the window.

Maybe Kaarlo was wrong and this Farm isn't a Misery. Maybe it's a Fortune after all.

Wilbert, I say, maybe we can be the Fortunates instead of the Miserables.

May, he says with a yawn, all I want to be is Asleep.

CHAPTER FIVE

The Most Wicked Place

Pappa decides to go in on the Stanley venture. He tells us at breakfast and by lunchtime, he's had me translate the paperwork Mr. Yerrington left behind three times. When Pappa's finally satisfied that he understands everything, he nods.

Joo, he says. This is the answer to our troubles.

I pick up the pen to sign his name but he shakes his head and signs it himself. He never went to proper school, but he can still sign his name.

Jalmer Jackson

These are dreaming days for all us Jackson children for now we can see what might be, like a blue sky or a warm breeze. The rain and storms and mud are forgotten and we're dry as can be and full of hope for the future.

Kaarlo is like a condemned man who has been unexpectedly pardoned.

Finally, he says. Finally I can make my own way.

Maybe you can get your ears fixed now, I tell Wendell.

What'd you say? he asks.

Maybe You Can Get Your Ears Fixed!

You don't have to shout, he says.

What do you want, May? Isaiah asks, and it's not even a question in my mind.

New Shoes! I say.

Trying to impress Berle? Wilbert asks.

Berle? I say.

He's sweet on you.

There's nothing sweet about Berle, I say.

Or you, Wilbert says with a knowing sniff. When's the last time you had a bath?

Mr. Yerrington comes by a few days later to collect the papers. He gives Pappa some fancy-looking Stock Certificates in the Stanley Company.

Put them somewhere safe, he advises Pappa.

And then almost as an afterthought, he pulls some money out of his pocket and hands it to Pappa.

A token of our appreciation, Mr. Yerrington says.

Pappa counts it and looks up, shocked. A hundred dollars! Pappa says.

You are our partner now. Mr. Yerrington winks at me. Buy a pretty dress for your little girl here.

That's a waste of good money, I say, but Mr. Yerrington just laughs.

That night we sit around the kitchen table staring at the stock certificates and the money. I've never seen so much money in my whole life and Pappa says this is just the beginning.

Should we build a new barn, Jalmer? Mamma asks.

Pappa's eyes soften and then he says something I never in all my born years expected him to say.

The barn can wait, he says. First thing we get is a boughten dress for you.

Oh, Jalmer, Mamma says and leans forward and kisses him.

I never did understand how she could kiss such a scratchy beard, but she don't seem to mind one bit.

Pappa takes us shopping in Astoria. Astoria has dance halls and gambling parlors and opium dens and saloons and bawdy houses. Folks says it is the

Most Wicked Place on Earth and that you can't walk down the street without meeting the Devil himself. I don't know about the Devil, but I can't wait to see Aunt Alice, who is Mamma's sister.

Astoria is across the Columbia River and it is a boat ride from Nasel, so Uncle Aarno takes us on the *General Custer*. Poor Isaiah must remain behind on the farm to mind the animals.

You mortgaged the farm, Jalmer? Uncle Aarno asks.

Joo, Pappa says.

I could have helped you out if you needed it, my uncle says to my father.

Pappa's lips tighten and Uncle Aarno sighs.

You're more stubborn than she was, Uncle Aarno mutters under his breath.

Uncle Aarno and Pappa were Best Brothers once, like me and Wilbert. But then Grandma Patience died and she left everything to Uncle Aarno and nothing to anyone else. Pappa has never forgiven his mamma for this, especially since we were the ones who took her in at the end and she was mean as a snake. But like Wilbert said, it's just like her to cause trouble, even Dead.

Astoria rises on a hill, the houses like pretty little eggs perched on hay. The docks are crowded with ships from faraway places. The gold rush here comes not from digging in the ground but from harvesting the sea. Fortunes are made in salmon and oysters.

We walk along taking in the sights. Ladies in beautiful skirts of blue and red and gold linger in doorways, smiling. There is a show playing at the Casino that features Juanita and Minnette in Their Wondrous Serpentine Dance. A bird with feathers the colors of the rainbow squawks from a cage hung outside a window. When we pass, the bird whistles lustily and says, Hey, Pete! What you doing down there! Come on up and enjoy yourself!

I turn to Wilbert and say, Wicked Places sure are a lot more exciting than Nasel!

When we walk through the part of town where the Chinamen live, Mamma looks around nervously, eyeing the women in their loose dresses.

They're all so strange, she says.

Pappa takes us to a dry goods store and tells us that we may each pick out one thing.

Wendell goes straight to the counter where there is a small selection of books.

Alvin and Ivan choose matching hats.

Wilbert picks a new belt of soft leather.

Kaarlo slides a coat on, looking at himself in the mirror.

Mamma picks out a fancy dress for herself, and a shirt for Pappa.

Can I help you, miss? the storekeeper asks me.

Do you have any shoes? I ask.

Certainly, he says, and pulls some out. These just came in last week from San Francisco.

I sit on a stool and the man slides them on my feet. They're polished black, high with little buttons down the front. They're beautiful and they fit my feet like a second skin.

They're the very latest fashion. All the ladies in Paris are wearing them, the man tells me.

What about the ladies in Nasel? I ask.

Pappa pays the man with the new money, and when I walk out of the store, my feet float on the plank-board walkway.

Then everyone heads off in their own direction. Kaarlo says he wants to see a friend, and Alvin and Ivan mumble something about pretty girls, and Wendell says he just wants to wander around alone. Wilbert and me have plans of our own.

Be sure to be at Aunt Alice's for supper, Mamma says.

Pappa shouts after us, And Stay Away From The Wicked Places!

Wilbert and me race down an alley straight to the back door of Mariah's Tavern, the most notorious saloon in all of Astoria. Everyone says that Mariah had her own husband shanghaied to get rid of him. I don't care if she did. She makes the best corn fritters in the whole world.

As I live and breathe, Mariah drawls. If it isn't May Amelia Jackson.

The Widow Mariah has a long single braid of white hair going down her back, and rumor has it that she keeps her money in the stockings on her legs.

Hiya, Mariah! I say.

What about me? Wilbert asks.

I am full to the gills with men around here, Wilbert. It's very rare I get to see a young lady like your sister here.

I ain't no lady, I say.

How've you children been? she asks.

We've been wet, I say. We live in Nasel.

She chuckles.

Hi, May! Hi, Wilbert! a voice says and I whirl and see a brown-haired boy sitting on a rough stool, a plate of fritters balanced on his knee.

It's my old friend, Otto Cheng. Otto's a Chinaman, but he speaks English and Finn, too. He's the smartest boy I ever met and he knows all the good places for adventure in Astoria.

Otto! I say. What are you doing here?

Where else would I be? he asks. I can't resist Mariah's fritters.

Mariah rolls her eyes at Otto and says, He was here this morning, too.

Those *are* mighty tasty-looking fritters, I say.

Mariah mock-groans and says, Oh, go on and take some. I don't turn away drunk sailors; I won't turn away hungry children.

We fill our bellies with the fritters fresh from the oven. They're so good that I imagine if I died and went to heaven, the clouds would be full of Mariah's fritters.

Mariah admires my new shoes.

My, what fine shoes, Mariah says. You find Old Landsman's treasure?

Mr. Landsman was one of the first settlers in the area, and he buried his gold somewhere but nobody's ever been able to find it.

Pappa invested in the Stanley Company and we're rich now, I say.

What company is that?

The one that's building the new town! Pappa bought me these shoes and They're The Latest Paris Fashion!

She laughs and says, And they go perfectly with your overalls.

Out in the barroom, someone is raising a ruckus. A glass breaks and a man shouts, It ain't right! These Chinamen take jobs from honest men!

Another yells, All Chinamen Should Go Home!

Mariah's lips thin and she opens the door and hollers, If you men don't settle down, I'm getting Big Ben.

The room goes hush-quiet and I hear murmured apologies.

Mariah gives us a satisfied look.

Works every time, she says.

Big Ben must be a real scary fellow, I say.

Oh, believe me, he is, she says, and nods at the wall behind her where there's a rifle on a shelf.

Someone's carved in it: BIG BEN.

Otto takes us to the cannery where his parents work. His daddy is the foreman. It's not hard to miss if you've got a nose. Just follow the smell of fish guts.

The inside of the cannery is buzzing with knives chopping and fish parts flying everywhere. This one cans salmon, which is real popular with folks back East. I think if I worked in here, I wouldn't ever want to eat a bite of salmon again. The workers are mostly men, although there are some women. It is one of the few places a respectable lady can work around here. It is also the stinkiest, slimiest place I have ever seen in my life. I'd rather muck out a hundred cow stalls than work here.

There's my mother, Otto says.

We go over to Otto's mother's table. It's her job

to cut off the head and the tail and the fins of the salmon and she does it right quick. The fella next to her takes out the guts, and the next one the scales. By the time they're finished with the fish, you never even would've guessed that it once swam in the Columbia.

Otto's mamma says something to Otto in Chinese. She's just like Pappa and Mamma; she can't speak English. It's up to all us children to do the talking.

My mother says that she likes your shoes, May Amelia, Otto says.

They're the latest Paris fashion, I say, and when Otto translates back to his mother, she gives me a wry look and says something to Otto.

Mamma wants to know if the ladies from Paris stand in fish guts, too?

After that, Otto takes us to the spot of a recent murder. It's near the water, in a dangerous part of Astoria. Not that that stops us.

That's where it happened, Otto says, pointing to an outhouse sitting on planks not far from a rooming house. There is a geranium set in front of the outhouse.

He got shot in the outhouse? I ask.

No, Otto says. The outhouse *murdered* him!

Otto explains that the man was doing his business when the rotten planks broke and he fell into the water below and drowned.

That sure would be a bad way to die, Wilbert says with a low whistle.

Otto admires Wilbert's belt. I like your belt.

Just got it, Wilbert replies.

So your family is rich now? Otto asks.

We will be, I say. We got the stock papers.

My father says you are not a rich man unless you hold money in your hand, Otto says.

Mr. Yerrington said the stock papers are worth a quarter of a million dollars, I say.

Who's Mr. Yerrington? Otto asks.

The man from the Stanley Company, I say.

Otto raises an eyebrow. Papers worth that much money? It sounds too good to be true.

You don't understand, Otto, I say. It is Different here in America.

Aunt Alice lives in a pretty house on the hill. She hasn't got herself a husband, but she has a Gentleman Friend who does not live with her and buys her all sorts of fine things. Far as I can tell, it's better to have a Gentleman Friend than a Husband. Pappa doesn't approve of Aunt Alice, but then he doesn't approve of much.

There you children are! We were getting worried! she exclaims when she opens the door.

My aunt is very beautiful, with her silk dresses

and her hair twisted in a cunning knot. She has lived here for so long that Mamma says she is a City Girl and wouldn't know how to milk a cow if she had to. If I could live in a house like this, I wouldn't mind one bit if I never milked a cow again.

Supper is a festive occasion. Aunt Alice is always cooking American-style dishes from Mrs. Fannie Farmer's cookbook. Tonight she has made beef stew with dumplings, chicken potpie, potato curls, and bread and butter pudding. Pappa prefers Finn food, but I don't care none if the food is American. It's Delicious.

Mamma tells Aunt Alice all about Pappa investing in the Stanley Company.

How thrilling! My aunt claps. You've both worked so hard.

I've worked hard, too! I say.

Hard at being stinky, Ivan says. What is that terrible smell?

I got fish guts on my shoes when we visited Otto's mother at the cannery, I say.

The canneries are having a lot of accidents, Aunt Alice says. Those poor Chinamen.

Dirty work, Pappa agrees.

Kaarlo says, I've been thinking. Why don't we open an oyster cannery of our own when the money from the stocks comes in? With some of the Finn men? We give everybody a share.

Pappa looks at Kaarlo appraisingly.

We'll see, Pappa says, which is the closest thing to a Yes Kaarlo will ever get.

Kaarlo looks down, but I know he is smiling.

It grows dark and Aunt Alice takes me out to the porch. We watch the lamplighter move along the streets lighting the gas lamps and soon Astoria twinkles like the sky above.

My aunt stares out into the night and says, It looks like your life is changing, my dear.

Maybe Pappa will let us move here to Astoria. I'm tired of living with so many boys, I tell her.

Aunt Alice arches her eyebrow, and says, My dear, there are boys everywhere. And every last one of them wants to find his fortune.

Are there that many fortunes to find? I ask.

For every lucky man who gets rich, there are a hundred who don't, she says and shrugs.

It's a good thing then that Pappa's one of the lucky ones!

She smiles down at me. You are such a dear, dear girl. You deserve every happiness in the world.

I'd settle for my own bed, I say.

The Devil You Know

This morning in church, the preacher talked about the Devil, and how the Devil Has Been Wandering Around Nasel, and how we best Watch Out and not be taken in by His Tricks.

Wilbert, I say. Why would the Devil want to come to Nasel, where all it does is rain? You'd think he'd want to be somewhere hotter.

Maybe he likes the saunas, Wilbert says.

After church, Wilbert and me take the rowboat and go fishing. We set out our lines where the fishies are fat and lazy.

I'm gonna ask Pappa if I can go to the sauna on Saturday night, Wilbert says.

Finns like saunas and Saturday night is Sauna Night around here. The men go over to Mr. Petersen's and take their sauna. Young boys like Wilbert aren't allowed to join the men's sauna until they grow up and have beards.

You ain't got no whiskers, I tell him.

I got one right here, he insists, pointing to his chin, which is bare as a baby's bottom.

Why do you want to go so bad anyhow? I ask him.

He frowns at me. To hear the talk, of course.

I can't imagine what talk that will be, seeing as Finn men ain't very good at talking to begin with. One time Pappa's cousin Isaak came to visit from Finland. Pappa hadn't seen him since he was a boy. When he finally saw Isaak all he said was Glad to See You, Isaak, and Isaak said Likewise, Jalmer, and then they sat in the parlor smoking pipes and saying nothing. You'd think you'd have something to say after forty years but I Guess Not.

We catch three fish only and when we get home we leave our bucket by the front door along with our muddy shoes. Mamma is sitting at the table slicing potatoes.

Mamma, I says, we caught three fish!

We'll have them for supper, she says. Go on and clean them up for me, please.

But when we go back outside, there is no sign of the fish anywhere.

Maybe the Devil took them! I say.

Wilbert goes behind the henhouse and says, The Devil took them all right.

And there's Bosie eating our fish.

The Devil sure is furry, I say.

Wilbert's got his heart set on going to the men's sauna, and asks Pappa.

You're Just a Boy, son.

I ain't no boy, Wilbert grumbles to me.

Why don't we just sneak up and listen in on them? I say, and Wilbert grins at me.

We wait till all the men are in the sauna and then slip over and sit outside, listening. They talk about the price for cream and what's the best way to get rid of bunions. But mostly they talk about how they would give anything for a good pair of socks because there's nothing worse than cold wet feet when you're trying to chop down a tree. It's so boring I may as well be in church.

Any news of your niece and nephew? Mr. Petersen asks.

I hear Pappa's gruff voice and am surprised.

Someone's supposed to be bringing them over, Pappa says.

The Trouble with May Amelia

High price to pay to come to America, Mr. Clayton adds.

How'd they catch him anyway? Kaarlo asks.

The Devil never bothered to throw out his bloody clothes, Pappa says. Just hid 'em in his hayloft.

My ears prick up at Devil and I whisper to Wilbert, What're they talking about?

He shrugs and a moment later the door slams open and a bunch of naked men walk out, their behinds as bright as the full moon shining down on them.

If the Devil was here, he's scared away now after seeing that sight for sure!

I am spooning out dessert for everyone—*riisipuuro*—when there's a knock at the door.

Two children thin as shadows are standing there, the preacher behind them. The little girl isn't more than three and has white-blond hair that's tied back in a dirty braid. The boy has a thick woolly scarf wrapped around his neck almost to his chin and is so thin that there's not enough meat on him to feed a sparrow.

Your folks home? the preacher asks me.

Mamma! Pappa! I call. Preacher's here.

Mamma gasps when she sees the little girl. Ana's children? she asks, and tears start running down her face.

70

They showed up on a boat in Astoria, the preacher says. When I went by their father's place, he wasn't there.

He had to go to Seattle to take care of some business, Pappa says, stepping forward. Won't be back for a week or so. I don't think he was expecting them yet.

Boat got in early, the preacher explains.

My mother can't stop staring at the little girl.

She looks just like Ana did at that age, Mamma says.

Can they stay here until their father comes back? the preacher asks Pappa.

'Course, he says.

My mother shoos the children inside, saying Oh, you poor things! Come in where it's warm.

They stand awkwardly in the parlor looking around with curious eyes.

Did they bring anything with them? Mamma asks the preacher and he replies, Just the clothes on their back.

Judging by the smell, the clothes have been on their back for a long time. They stink worse than the milk tureens when they've been left in the sun.

Mamma sizes up both children and says, I'll go find some clean clothes. May Amelia, you give them something to eat.

The children follow me into the kitchen and the little girl climbs onto a bench and the boy sits next to Wilbert. I fix up two bowls of riisipuuro and bring them over. The girl eats hers so fast that we children just stare at her. I've never seen anyone eat that fast before, and I live with boys.

You want some more? I ask and she nods and I fill her bowl again and it disappears just as fast and she holds out her bowl.

More, she says, so I fill it again.

Meanwhile, the boy's not even lifting his spoon. He just keeps looking around, his eyes fixing on Bosie who's licking clean a bucket of dirty dishes.

For this? the boy says with disgust.

You don't like *riisipuuro*? I ask. I can put some more sugar on it if you want.

For This Is Why We Come From Finland? he practically spits out. This place in the middle of nowhere?

The boys and I look at each other, but no one says anything.

The girl holds out her empty bowl.

You want more? I ask her.

More! she demands.

And then she makes a face and opens her mouth and every bit of *riisipuuro* she ate comes back up, all over the front of me.

Kaarlo shakes his head, and says, I Think She's Had Enough.

The dirty children turn out to be our cousins, Helmi and Jaakko. They are Uncle Niihlo's kids and they have come to America without their mother because she has died, although nobody will say how.

Mamma finds an old dress of mine for Helmi and Jaakko fits just fine into a pair of Wilbert's overalls, but he refuses to take off his filthy scarf. He wears it twined tightly around his neck no matter the time of day and even sleeps with it on. He is nervous and quiet-like and reminds me of a cow that's been spooked.

Mamma gives Jaakko and Helmi my and Wilbert's old bedroom. It has a nice view of the Nasel, but Jaakko doesn't seem pleased. If he thinks our place is bad, just wait until he sees Uncle Niihlo's cabin. It is little more than a shack, what the men call a Bachelor House, just raw wood floors, no rugs, no curtains, and a mattress stuffed with straw.

Wilbert and me sleep in with Wendell and Isaiah. I wake up in the middle of the night and make my way to the outhouse in the dark. When I walk back in the house I hear a *swoosh* and a fire poker is flying at me. I dodge, tumbling to the floor. When I look up, Jaakko is standing over me brandishing the poker and breathing heavily.

Don't hit me! I say.

What were you doing out there?

I was just using the outhouse! I tell him, but he doesn't lower the poker.

I heard a noise, he insists. Someone's out there.

That was me.

He doesn't look convinced. But before I can say anything else, Pappa comes stomping into the room. He takes in the scene, and barks at Jaakko, Put Down That Poker, Son!

Jaakko's hands open and the poker falls to the floor with a clatter.

What are you children doing out of bed? Pappa demands.

I heard someone outside, Jaakko says in a low voice.

It was just me using the outhouse! I tell Pappa.

Pappa looks at Jaakko with pity in his eyes and says, Go To Bed. It will be morning soon enough.

The boys and I are on our way to the schoolhouse and I tell them about what happened during the night with Jaakko, and they look between each other and I know they are keeping a secret from me because they are terrible secret keepers.

Finally Isaiah says, May as well tell her. She'll find out soon enough with her Big Ears.

I ain't got big ears, I say. What's the secret?

That Aunt Ana was murdered in cold blood! Wendell blurts out.

You can't even hear, and you knew before me? I ask.

You're a girl, May, he says. We didn't want to scare you.

Nothing scares me, I say.

Isaiah goes on to tell me the Terrible Tale. Aunt Ana had sold their house in Finland so that she and the children might finally join Uncle Niihlo. On the night before they were to set sail to come to America, someone broke into their house and stabbed Aunt Ana and Jaakko with a hunting knife and left them for dead and took all the money from the sale of the house. When a friend came by in the morning to take them to the dock, he found Ana dead and Jaakko barely alive and little Helmi hiding in a closet.

Jaakko got stabbed all around his neck, Wilbert says. That's why he wears that scarf all the time.

And here I was just thinking he was cold.

Helmi is playful with the boys, but Jaakko doesn't want anything to do with us children. The only soul he can bear near him is Bosie, and Bosie seems to like

Jaakko, too. Our scruffy dog trails after our strange cousin wherever he goes.

Jaakko's eyes never stop moving and now I know it is because he is looking for the Devil to come out of the darkness and finish the job. He jumps at every noise and his back is never turned to the door no matter what room he is in. And he doesn't sleep, not one wink. We all hear him pacing the house at night. The circles under his eyes are thick smudges of gray.

We Gotta Do Something, I say to Wilbert.

What's there to do? Wilbert says. His daddy will be here any day now. He'll take care of him.

But I'm not waiting on Uncle Niihlo.

Breakfast has been cleared and there is no school today, so I say to Jaakko, You want to come fishing with me? We can catch supper?

He hesitates, and Mamma says, That's a lovely idea, May Amelia. And you'll catch more with two fishermen.

I'll come, Jaakko says reluctantly.

Bosie comes, too, hopping into the rowboat after Jaakko.

It is a beautiful day—no rain, just a soft warm wind, all sweet-smelling and green. You can almost hear summer tumbling down the mountains. I row to the Baby Island, but when we get there I don't pick up our fishing poles.

I want to show you something, I say, and I take him to the old sorcerer tree.

What's this? he asks.

You can sleep here, I say.

Sleep? he echoes.

This is the safest place ever, I explain. Even the Devil can't get you here.

The Devil? He gives a sharp laugh. I ain't worried about the Devil. I'm more worried about that fellow who lives next to you. The one with the hand.

You mean our neighbor, Mr. Clayton?

He nods.

Mr. Clayton would never hurt you, I tell him.

But Jaakko's eyes are stark with fear. My Neighbor was the one who killed my mother and tried to kill me!

Your neighbor? I whisper.

I knew him. I went to church with him.

I shake my head.

And it could happen again here, my cousin says, his eyes full of worry. You never know what your neighbors are gonna do.

Our neighbors are real nice, I say. Mr. Clayton bakes good pies, too.

Jaakko shakes his head, and says, You can't tell from looking at a person.

The breeze blows.

No neighbors here on the Baby Island, I say. And nobody knows about the sorcerer tree except me and Wilbert.

He stares at the tree, his face pinched. Bosie licks Jaakko's hand.

Go on, I say. Me and Bosie will watch over you.

I expect him to say No, but he just nods wearily.

My cousin Jaakko curls up in the old sorcerer tree and closes his eyes and Sleeps.

Uncle Niihlo arrives the next morning to fetch his children. Jaakko flies into his daddy's arms and hugs him tight.

My boy, Uncle Niilho weeps. My brave, brave boy.

But when my uncle holds out his arms to Helmi, she clings to Mamma's skirts.

Oh, Helmi, Uncle Niihlo says, his eyes wet. You look just like your sweet mother. Come give Pappa a hug.

Helmi whimpers, her eyes fearful.

Uncle Niihlo looks at Mamma. I don't think she remembers me. She was just a babe when I came here.

Mamma says, She's been through a lot.

Maybe it would be best if she stayed a spell with you, Uncle Niihlo says. Can you keep her for a bit longer?

Of course, Mamma says a little too quickly. We can keep them both if you'd like.

No, my boy comes with me, he says, his arm tight around his son.

You want to borrow Bosie? I ask Jaakko.

Borrow?

Looks like we're borrowing your sister for a while, I say. Bosie's loud. Barks up a storm if anyone comes near the house.

He hesitates for a moment and then he says, I'll take good care of him.

I know, I say.

Uncle Niihlo rows smoothly across the water, Bosie yipping away.

Why'd you give him our dog? Wilbert asks after they leave.

He's just borrowing him, I say.

What's he need him for?

To scare away the Devil, I say.

CHAPTER SEVEN

The Sweetest Child Ever

Helmi settles into our house as comfortably as one of Buttons's own kittens. She's playful as one, too—running and chattering and smiling her big smile. All the boys dote on her, picking her up and tickling her just to hear her giggle. It's like they've never seen a little girl before.

Wendell, who's always been the best seamstress in the family, sews Helmi dresses out of homespun and Isaiah brings her a baby chick. Ivan and Alvin build her a little wagon and pull her around in the dirt until she squeals. Kaarlo, who never has a kind word for anyone, hoists her up on his shoulders and walks her out to the fields and shows her the cows and the tidelands and the Nasel.

Mamma spends hours braiding and brushing Helmi's hair until it gleams like fresh milk. She gives Helmi a little stool to stand on in the kitchen next to her. Helmi stirs empty pots like she's trying to cook. The truth is, Mamma can hardly bear to let Helmi out of her sight.

Even Pappa is charmed by her. He calls her *Kukka* which means Flower and she calls him *Faari* which means Grandfather. She runs up to him and he growls at her like a cranky old bear, but she just tugs on his whiskers until he belly-laughs and tosses her into the air.

Oh, my, but she is such a good little girl, Mamma says.

And it's true. There never was a sweeter child than Helmi, except maybe my sister, Amy, but she never got a chance to grow up, which surely don't seem fair and nobody seems to remember except Me.

Helmi has our old room all to herself while the rest of us are crammed in like oysters in a tin. Mamma says Helmi's been through a lot and Deserves Some Peace. I want to say that I been through a whole lot, too, and I Deserve My Own Bed, especially considering how loud Wilbert snores.

How long do you think Helmi is going to stay here? I ask Wilbert.

He looks at me and says, Why, what did she do?

She ain't done nothing. She's good! She never causes a speck of trouble! Even Pappa thinks she's sweet as sugar!

His eyes narrow. May, are you jealous?

'Course I ain't jealous. She's just a baby.

Helmi is in bed and we are all sitting in the parlor. Pappa is reading his Finnish-American newspaper and Mamma is knitting socks for Alvin and Ivan.

I ask Mamma, Was I a sweet baby?

Pappa snorts.

You were a little fussy, May Amelia, Mamma says gently.

Pappa says, I used to put you in the barn.

In the barn? I ask. Why?

You never stopped crying. At least that way we got some sleep.

I think she liked the cows, Isaiah says in a dreamy voice.

She still smells like them, Ivan snickers.

You were born irritating, May Amelia, Alvin says.

And you haven't changed a bit, Ivan adds.

* * *

Helmi starts carrying around a doll with a delicate china face and wearing a blue silk dress.

Where did she get that doll? I ask Mamma, for we have no other girls here, and it's not mine. My Susannah is a sturdy rag doll who wants to be a pirate.

Mamma looks down and says, It was Amy's.

Amy? I gasp.

Your father bought it for her when she was born.

But Mamma, I say. How could you give her Amy's doll?

May Amelia, Helmi has nothing. She lost her mother. She's in a strange land. Your sister would have wanted her to have some small comfort.

No she wouldn't have! I say. Amy never even got to hold it!

I'm not going to discuss this anymore, May Amelia, Mamma says.

Pappa goes to Astoria to do business and when he returns he is carrying a package. Usually he gets us children a treat, like candy or maybe an orange. I am so excited I go running up to him.

Did you bring us anything, Pappa? I ask.

He stares down at me but before he can answer little Helmi runs up to him shouting, Faari! Faari!

He kneels down in front of her and she tugs on his beard and squeals with laughter.

Gotcha something, Kukka, he says and opens the package and holds out the prettiest little straw hat I ever did see. It is trimmed with a black velvet ribbon.

Helmi tries it on and spins around in it happily.

Then he pauses and looks at me and digs in his pocket and holds out a handful of lemon drops.

You like these ones, right?

I nod and take them. Thanks, Pappa, I say.

Then my father takes Helmi's hand and says, Let's go show Mother how pretty you look, and they walk to the house hand in hand.

The lemon drops taste sour on my tongue.

Mamma is boiling laundry and she says, May Amelia, go play with little Helmi.

But Helmi is no kind of playmate. She isn't interested in throwing manure patties or climbing trees or fishing. All my life I've dreamed of having another little girl to play with, and now that I've got one, she's no fun at all. She wanders around the farm in her pretty new hat and I follow her to where Pappa does his horseshoeing. She picks up an old horseshoe and looks at it.

That's a horseshoe, I say.

Her face lights up.

Shoe! she says. Shoe!

Then she brings the horseshoe right down on my foot and laughs.

I'm as startled as if I've fallen into the Nasel. I look down at my foot and back up at Helmi, who's laughing likes it's the funniest thing ever. I know she's a baby but she just hit me with a horseshoe and she did it on purpose! I don't even think, I just yank the hat off her head and crush it on the ground under my feet. She starts wailing away, loud enough to scare every cow away.

Wilbert's walking toward us and he saw the whole thing.

May! Wilbert says. What'd you do that for?

She Hit Me With A Horseshoe!

But she's a Baby!

It Was A Horseshoe! I say.

When I show Mamma the bloody bruise on my foot, she won't hear a word against Helmi.

You're a big girl, May Amelia, she says. You should have moved your foot.

Helmi is standing at the hog pen looking in and she says, Want To Ride!

The boys are always riding the hogs. The hogs can be wild, but then so can my brothers.

Ride! Ride! she pleads.

You want to ride the hogs? I ask.

Yes! Yes! she says and I say, Fine, fine.

I lift her up over the fence and drop her down onto a fat slow hog's back. She tumbles off the hog and starts wailing away. The poor hogs are so startled by her ruckus that they start snorting and bumping into each other and that just makes Helmi shriek and shriek and shriek. Who knew a little girl could make so much noise?

Be quiet! I yell at her. You're riling up the hogs!

But she doesn't listen and just wails louder so I open the door to the pen to get to her but she's got the hogs so worked up that they rush me and knock me over, too, and take off from the pen in all directions. That's when everyone except Wendell comes running—Kaarlo Ivan Alvin Isaiah Wilbert Mamma Pappa. Wendell's just lucky he's deaf and can't hear her shrieking her head off.

Kukka! Pappa bellows and leaps into the middle of the pen and grabs up Helmi and passes her to Mamma.

The hogs are loose! Kaarlo shouts.

Mamma rocks Helmi, saying soothingly over and over again *äitin tyttö*, which means mother's girl and I feel my heart clench.

What Happened? Pappa demands.

She wanted to ride a hog and then she started hollering and she scared 'em!

Pappa looks like he's going to explode.

You put her in the pen with the hogs?

I was being nice to her, like Mamma said!

Honestly, girl, You Have No Sense, and he carries Helmi's trembling body back to the house.

It takes most of the afternoon to round up the hogs, and we don't find one until the next day. It ran all the way over to Jacob Clayton's farm and nosed its way into his house and ate a pie.

Helmi's no worse for the wear after her wild ride, but Pappa is so angry with me he practically turns red every time he sees me. Even Wilbert gives me a look, a Real You've Gone And Done It Again May Amelia look, and I know I am well and truly in Trouble. For my punishment, I must empty slop jars in the morning which is where a body goes if they cannot make it to the outhouse during the night.

After church on Sunday, Uncle Niihlo and Jaakko come back to our house for lunch. Helmi won't go near her father. She sits next to Mamma the whole time, and buries her face in my mother's skirts.

I think she just needs a little more time, Mamma says to Uncle Niihlo.

Jaakko goes outside and I follow him. We stand on the fence around the hog pen. Jaakko's cheeks

seem fuller. Mamma always said Finland was Starv-
ing Country and that she never knew what a full
belly was until she came to America.

When is your daddy gonna take Helmi back? I
ask him.

I guess when he finds us a new mamma, he says.
Got no one else to mind her.

Ain't no eligible women here in the valley except
for Miss McEwing our teacher, I tell him. Why can't
you watch her?

Pappa wants me to start going to the schoolhouse.
Says I have to learn English or I'll never fit in.

Nearly everybody speaks Finn, I say.

I just want to go home, he says.

Do You Miss Your Mamma?

He looks down at the ground and then up at me
and there is a haunted look in his eyes.

I don't miss the last time I saw her, he whispers.
But I miss every time before that.

The boys are out in the fields and Mamma is in the
kitchen. I am taking the slop jars out to the outhouse. When I come back past the garden, there is
the little doll, the little doll that was meant for my sister, and it's lying in the mud where Helmi has left it,
its pretty dress ruined and I can't bear it, I just can't.

I grab it and jump into the rowboat and go to

the Smith Island where my baby sister sleeps forever. I'm gonna hide it where that Helmi will never find it, where she will never ruin it. I sit on Amy's grave and I show her the doll because she needs to know that there was a doll for her, a doll that some other little girl played with before she even had the chance. She needs to know that she isn't forgotten now that there's a pretty girl who is sweet and makes Pappa smile running through the house.

I'll Never Forget You, I tell her, and the wind blows and I swear for certain sure she whispers back to me.

She says, I Know, May.

I am washing the breakfast dishes the next morning when Helmi runs around the kitchen saying, No Doll! No Doll!

Mamma shakes her head and says, I have no idea where she put that doll. I've looked everywhere for it.

It'll turn up, Pappa says.

I'm done my chores, Mamma, I say. Can I go fishing?

As long as you weed the potato patch, she says.

Sure, sure, I say. I won't forget the potato patch.

It's a fine day for fishing and I've just set my line in the water to catch some fishies when Berle comes running past me.

Better Pull In Your Line, May Amelia! They're splashing now!

Okay, I say.

And he keeps right on running past me, shouting Logs-a-coming! Logs-a-coming!

I pull in my line and go back to the house.

Mamma's in the kitchen darning socks and she looks surprised when I walk in the door.

I thought you were fishing, May Amelia, Mamma says.

They're releasing the splash dam, I say.

Mamma goes still. Where's Helmi? she asks.

I shrug. I don't know.

Mamma runs outside, shouting Helmi! Helmi!

But the little girl doesn't answer and Mamma runs over to where Pappa is looking at a horse's hoof.

Jalmer! They've released the splash dam! I can't find Helmi!

My father turns pale and hollers, Boys!

We tear the farm apart, looking for little Helmi. We search everywhere from the cowshed to the hayloft but it's too late: the logs are already crashing down with the raging water.

Not again, Mamma sobs.

And all I can think is that my sweet sister Amy is lying dead and buried on the Smith Island and I can't bear it if another little girl is laid in the ground beside her. I run along the river shouting her name.

Helmi! I cry.

The crashing logs are the saddest sound I have ever heard.

Everyone goes back to the house and sits around the kitchen table. Mamma is red-eyed and Pappa has his face in his hands.

I reckon I'll weed the potato patch now, I say, but no one answers.

I get my bucket and go out to the potato patch and that's when I see her:

Helmi is curled fast asleep on the soil.

When I walk in the door holding Helmi's hand, Mamma bursts into tears.

Where did you find her? Isaiah asks.

I didn't know we planted little girls in the potato patch this year, I say.

The potato patch? Mamma asks.

Pappa looks at me and crinkles his eyes.

May Amelia, he says, you were the best crop we ever put in.

CHAPTER EIGHT

Learning Is Dangerous Here

Rain comes to the valley and still we must go to the schoolhouse. Miss McEwing says even the weather cannot stop learning.

We children pile in the rowboat, and by the time we reach the schoolhouse, we are sopping wet.

I Didn't Fall In The Water, I say to Miss McEwing when we walk in the door. It Fell On Me.

You weren't the only one, she says.

Every child in the room is wearing their under-drawers. All the damp clothes are hanging by the pot-belly stove, drying.

Take off your wet things and set them by the stove, Miss McEwing says. Hopefully they'll be dry by the time you go home.

Not much point if you ask me, I say. They'll just get wet again.

True enough, Miss McEwing says. But that's the charm of living in Nasel.

A few days later, it rains hard again, and every child is being taught their letters and sums in their under-drawers while their clothes dry by the stove.

This time the rain even gets the best of Miss McEwing. Her pretty hair is plastered to her head and looks like a wet dead animal.

We're halfway through the first lesson when the school door opens. Jaakko is standing there, his scarf wrapped tight around his neck.

Miss McEwing smiles.

Welcome, she says.

Jaakko hesitates and then walks to the front of the room. He's carrying a Finn primer.

We have a new pupil joining us today, Miss McEwing announces. His name is Jaakko.

She needn't have bothered introducing him, seeing as every child in the valley has already heard about The Boy Who Didn't Die. It is the most exciting thing that's happened in Nasel since a bear got trapped in the Kitinoja sauna and scared Mrs. Kitinoja half to death.

Miss McEwing takes the Finn primer from Jaakko.

You won't be needing that here, she tells him and then says slowly, We Only Speak English In This Schoolhouse.

He turns and looks at me blankly.

You Can't Speak Finn Here, I say to him in Finn.

Every child laughs.

Miss McEwing groans and mutters, Honestly.

Then she hands Jaakko a slate and a piece of chalk.

Jaakko doesn't speak any English, she says. Who would like to sit next to him and help him?

Not one child raises their hand. Truth be told, some of the boys look a little scared.

Come now children, Miss McEwing says, tapping her foot.

I raise my hand and say, He Can Sit By Me.

Jaakko slides into the desk and looks around in wonder like he's never seen a schoolroom in his life and believe me there's nothing interesting about this schoolhouse.

Ain't you ever been to school before? I ask him.

Sure, Jaakko says. But it's different here.

What do you mean? I ask.

Well, for one thing, he says, we wear clothes to school back in Finland.

Uncle Aarno says there is no nosier race of people than the Finns and he should know because he delivers the mail. If a letter arrives from Finland, it will be opened and read by every soul in the valley before it reaches the hands of its addressee. Poor Erik Olsen was the last person to find out his wife had a baby.

It turns out that Finn boys are just as bad as their parents because every one of them wants to see Jaakko's neck. They stare at him while we eat lunch. I am sharing my food—*rieska* and squeaky cheese— with my cousin. All my uncle sent for him to eat was some salt pork.

Your daddy find anybody to marry yet? I ask.

He said that there's a pretty girl at the logging camp who cooks for the men, but she's got religion.

What's wrong with that? I ask.

He don't believe in God no more after what happened, Jaakko says. Me neither.

Sure doesn't seem like God Was Paying Attention, I agree.

How's Helmi? he asks.

She likes to sleep in the potato patch, I say. How's Bosie?

Good, he says. Did you know he can catch fish?

Best fisherdog around, I say.

I heard he had his head chopped off, Nuutti says loudly from across the yard.

You think that scarf's holding it on? Waino asks.

If you just show them, they'll leave you alone, I tell Jaakko.

I don't care what they think, he says.

Those boys are gonna make your life a misery for sure.

He rubs his neck and says, They can't do anything to me that hasn't been done worse already.

And I guess he's right.

Miss McEwing comes to school with the family she boards with, and if the tides are against them, she is late. Which is what must have happened today because when we arrive at the schoolhouse, all the children are standing outside waiting around.

I hate coming here, Berle grumbles.

Better than shoveling manure, I say.

Not much, he says.

My cousin Jaakko is sitting by himself on a big stump. Nuutti walks right up to him with a smirk on his face.

I bet your neck's not even cut up at all, Nuutti says. I bet you made the whole thing up.

Jaakko just shrugs.

Prove it to us, Nuutti says.

Jaakko is pure Finn. He's got the emotion of a stone. All he does is blink at Nuutti.

Well? Nuutti asks.

Leave him alone, Nuutti, I say.

Nuutti grabs Jaakko's scarf and tries to pull it off, but Jaakko twists away.

Why you trying to take off Jaakko's scarf, Nuutti? Lonny asks. It's keeping him warm.

But Nuutti keeps tugging at the scarf.

I said leave him alone! I say, and I jump on Nuutti's back.

And then another boy tries to tear me off and Wilbert leaps in shouting That's My Sister and Lonny leaps on saying That's My Neighbor and Berle leaps in saying That's My May and then boys are piling on and it's worse than feeding time in a hog pen what with all the snuffling and smacking.

What Is Going On Here? a voice demands, and everyone looks up to see Miss McEwing standing over us.

The boys tumble away, leaving me and Jaakko on the muddy ground. Jaakko's still got his scarf on his neck, although it's looking a little worse for the wear.

May Amelia? my teacher demands.

We were just wrestling, Miss McEwing, I say. Honest.

Miss McEwing shakes her head. You are a horrible liar, May Amelia.

Yeah, but she sure can punch! Lonny says.

It's spelling time and I'm starting to see Berle's point of view. Not much use in knowing how to spell words on a farm. The cows don't care if we can spell "hay." All they want to do is eat it.

The first word is Destiny, Miss McEwing says. Write it out on your slates, children.

I copy it down, but no matter what any teacher tells you, it is more trying to read and write another language than to speak. You can just look at a body's face when they're talking to you and even if you don't know what they're saying, you know what they mean, especially if someone's yelling at you. Not to mention there are some words that don't translate real good. Like *sisu*. There ain't a word for *sisu* in English. Maybe that's why it's all Finns who live in this wet wilderness. You gotta have *sisu* to live here.

Now can anyone tell me what Destiny means? Miss McEwing asks.

Wendell's hand shoots up first as usual.

Yes, Wendell? Miss McEwing says.

Destiny is what's meant to be.

Very good, Wendell. Now can someone please use destiny in a sentence?

I raise my hand.

Miss McEwing raises an eyebrow. Yes, May Amelia?

It's my destiny to use the outhouse, I say.

All the boys laugh and Miss McEwing rolls her eyes.

Very amusing, Miss Jackson, she says. Anyone else?

I wave my hand. No, I say, it really is my destiny to use the outhouse. I Gotta Go! Bad!

You're excused, she says. And do try to think of a better sentence while you're out there.

I'm doing my business and thinking about Destiny when something strikes the outhouse and the whole thing shakes like it's caught in a storm.

Berle! I shout. Don't you dare!

I wait and That Something slams into the outhouse again.

Berle I Mean It! I holler loud as I can.

Then I peek out the outhouse and I know I have a heap more trouble than some boy trying to play a trick on me.

It's Friendly the bull!

He bellows and paws at the ground and looks mighty angry and I surely don't know why, seeing as this ain't *his* outhouse. Friendly charges straight at the outhouse and I slam the door shut.

Help! I cry but I guess everyone's too busy spelling fancy words to hear me.

The next thing I know Friendly hits the wobbly outhouse, and this time it tips right over with me in it. I fall and hit the ground, my arm catching on the wooden bench. And that's when I come up with a good sentence.

It Is My Destiny To Die In An Outhouse.

Friendly crashes into the outhouse again, pushing it, and all I can think is that this is one way of dying that even Uncle Aarno never thought of.

Run, May Amelia! a voice shouts.

I look out the door and see Jaakko circling around the schoolhouse, Friendly chasing after him. He's loosed his scarf and is waving it like a flag. All the other children and Miss McEwing are at the windows, watching with anxious faces.

Jaakko's rounding the schoolhouse for a second time, Friendly right behind him, when he sees me gaping at him.

Whatcha waiting for? he hollers at me. Run For It!

I can't make it to the schoolhouse door, so I just start running in the other direction. I run and run and run all the way to the Nasel. I jump in a rowboat and start rowing. When I reach the farm, Isaiah is the first brother I see and the last one I need.

Where are the other boys? I demand.

They're out in the back pasture. What's wrong? he asks.

Friendly's attacking the school! Everyone's inside! I'm the only one who got out! Get your gun!

By the time we return, Friendly is trying to break down the door of the schoolhouse. Friendly charges the door, and it cracks under his weight. But my gentle brother doesn't lift his gun.

Inside the little ones are crying.

Isaiah! I hiss.

A look settles over Isaiah's face, his lips tightening.

Fine, he says.

Isaiah whistles and Friendly rears about, nostrils flaring, and charges.

Blam!

The rifle fires and I expect to see Friendly lying in the dirt but he has turned tail and run off toward the Bakkila farm. All the children cheer.

Did I get him? Isaiah asks, looking bewildered.

No, but you scared him off, Isaiah! I say.

Miss McEwing opens the schoolhouse door and the children spill out, surrounding us. Berle rushes up to me, his face pale.

You okay, May? he asks, looking me over. His eyes widen in alarm when he takes in my arm.

You're hurt! he cries.

I'm fine, I say. It's just a scratch.

You could bleed to death!

I'm fine, Berle, I say. I've had worse.

But Berle just ignores me and strips off his shirt. He wraps it carefully around my arm, but he still doesn't look satisfied.

I'm gonna go fetch your mamma right now! And then he takes off running.

I'm Fine! I shout after him.

Wilbert chuckles.

Poor Berle, he says. He sure has got it bad.

Well done, Isaiah! Miss McEwing effuses, wringing her hands. I don't know what we would've done if you hadn't come along! You are a true hero!

Isaiah blushes. It was nothing, he says.

Looks like we're going to need a new outhouse, Miss McEwing says.

The outhouse is not the only thing the bull's torn up. Jaakko's ripped scarf is lying on the ground. Friendly's ruined it for good.

Where's Jaakko? I ask.

I'm down here! he calls from underneath the schoolhouse. He crawls out a moment later, all covered with cobwebs, but in one piece.

His neck is in plain view for everyone to see. Chunks of flesh are missing and the rest is a pink ribbon of scars. I've seen hogs butchered better. Miss

McEwing puts her hand over her mouth to stop her gasp.

Did someone try to chop your head off, Jaakko? Lonny asks.

They tried to, Jaakko says. But I got a strong neck.

Good thing, Lonny says.

The children laugh uneasily.

Then Jaakko looks at the shattered outhouse, and says, Learning Sure Is Dangerous Here In America.

CHAPTER NINE

Calving and Courting

There's no shortage of volunteers to help mend the damage that Friendly caused to the schoolhouse. The men trip over each other and every single one has his sights set on our pretty teacher.

First one to show up is tall Ben Armstrong. He brings a wagon full of lumber scraps.

I heard what happened, Ben says. Thought I could build you a new outhouse.

That's very kind of you, Miss McEwing says.

Next to come is Wild Cat Clark. He shows up with a dead cougar slung over one shoulder and drops it at Miss McEwing's feet.

Just killed it this morning, he says and she goes white. It'll make a mighty fine rug for under your desk.

How thoughtful, she says.

On and on they come. Even my cousin Thymei shows up and he's only got one eye.

Looks like she's running a bawdy house and not a schoolhouse, Pappa grumbles when he sees another man tying up his rowboat.

Miss McEwing smiles at every last one of them and after the outhouse is rebuilt and the door fixed she starts making little suggestions.

Oh, I do wish the children had a swing, she says loudly to Mr. Petersen and just like that we have a swing. Soon our schoolhouse is better than ever—we got a new outhouse, new desks, a swing, and a tall stack of neatly chopped wood to feed into the pot-belly stove. I almost expected one of the men to sew up some curtains for our windows.

Good thing she ain't married, Wilbert says, Or we'd be doing our sums in a shack.

It's calving time and our cows start dropping babies left and right. Since we have no barn, we must keep an eye on the poor calves to make sure they aren't eaten by cougars or bears. Pappa says every Jackson child must stay on the farm and help out and so there is no school for us. Our cow, Patience, decides to have her baby right as we're sitting down for supper.

Put on some coffee, May Amelia, Pappa says wearily.

I don't know what it is about babies that makes them come at the worst times. Mamma says it's because they've been sleeping so long in their mothers' bellies that they don't much care what time it is. I think they're just stubborn. And it looks like this calf is one of the most stubborn ones yet. It won't come out even though its mamma is groaning and mooing.

Come on old girl, Pappa urges the cow. Push that babe out.

Cow's just like your mother, Mamma says.

Finally, Pappa stands up, and shakes his head, and says, The babe's stuck.

He goes back to the house and when he returns, he has his gun.

Don't shoot her, Pappa! I plead.

She's suffering, girl.

What about Mr. Clayton? I suggest. He's got a good touch with animals.

Pappa wipes a hand over his forehead. Don't think he'll be able to do much, but can't see the harm in him trying. Go on and fetch him.

I'll go with you, May, Wilbert says.

Mr. Clayton answers the door on the second knock.

Calf coming? he asks.

How'd you know?

He chuckles. Saw that cow the other day. Looked about ready to drop.

When we get back to the farm, poor Patience is panting, her eyes glazed over. Mr. Clayton rolls up his sleeve and reaches his bare arm right up into the cow, up to the elbow. Just then Miss McEwing walks up to where we're all standing. She looks pretty and fresh.

Hiya, Miss McEwing! I say.

I was coming to see if you children were all right since you hadn't been to school, she says and then her mouth drops open when she sees Mr. Clayton with his arm up Patience.

Oh, My, she says.

Patience is having her baby and it's stuck. If Mr. Clayton can't get it out, Pappa's gonna have to shoot her, I explain.

Mr. Clayton glances back and says, Afternoon, ma'am.

Afternoon, she says, sounding flustered.

You think I might borrow a book sometime, ma'am? Mr. Clayton asks our teacher, twisting his arm up in Patience.

A *book?* she gasps.

I like to read after I take my supper, he says simply.

She blinks fast.

I have a few in my private collection that I can recommend, Miss McEwing says quickly. Why, I just read a wonderful novel by one Mr. Arthur Conan Doyle about a man named Sherlock Holmes and—

Patience lows as if to call attention to the fact that Mr. Clayton has his arm in her.

'Scuse me, ma'am, Mr. Clayton says to Miss McEwing, and then tugs and pulls and grunts. Finally, Mr. Clayton says, Got You Now, and Patience lets out a moo. The baby calf slides out all slippery and wet.

What are we gonna call the calf? Isaiah asks.

Let's call it Jacob, I say.

Long as you keep it as a milking cow, Mr. Clayton says with a twinkle in his eye. Don't be serving me for supper.

Then Mr. Clayton looks at Miss McEwing, and says, I'll be by for that book, ma'am.

Her eyes are glowing.

I'll look forward to it, she replies.

It's like Miss McEwing's under a spell because nothing seems to bother her anymore—not when little

Charles hides or even when I show up soaking wet on account of falling in the Nasel like always.

At lunchtime, Mr. Clayton drops by the schoolhouse and returns a book that Miss McEwing lent him.

I enjoyed it very much, he says.

Oh, I'm so glad! Miss McEwing says, her voice all breathy. I have another book I think you might like. Let me get it for you! And then she runs back inside.

You sure do like reading, huh, Mr. Clayton? I ask him.

His eyes sparkle at Miss McEwing's departing figure.

It has its attractions, he murmurs.

Miss McEwing returns and hands Mr. Clayton a book called *The War of the Worlds*.

This one is excellent, she says. It's by a very interesting author named H. G. Wells. I've never read anything like it before.

Thank you kindly, Mr. Clayton says, tips his hat, and walks away. Our teacher watches him the entire time. Her ears are bright red.

Berle says to me, We better start posting ads for a new teacher.

Why? I ask.

Because Miss McEwing's sweet on Mr. Clayton!

Mr. Clayton?

Didn't you see her ears?

You mean ears turning bright red means you're in love?

I don't know, he mumbles, and looks down, his ears bright red.

Mamma announces we're going to have some folks over for supper.

Who? I ask.

Mr. Clayton. And I thought I'd ask your teacher Miss McEwing.

Now I know that Berle was right after all. It ain't proper for an unmarried lady to have supper with an unmarried fellow, which is why they're going to have supper at our house so we can chaperone them.

I lay awake in bed all night tossing and turning. Miss McEwing's my favorite teacher ever. I can't bear to lose her.

Wilbert, I say, shaking my Best Brother awake.

I'm sleeping, he groans.

Wake up! We can't let him marry her! I say, poking him.

Berle asked you to marry him? Wilbert asks, blinking one eye open.

No! I say. Mr. Clayton's wooing Miss McEwing. He ain't right for her!

He flips over, and says, Seems like no fella is right for her in your opinion.

I Got To Stop Them, I say.

Wilbert pulls the covers over his head and says, The only thing You Got To Stop Is Waking Me Up.

The stew is bubbling on the stove when Mr. Clayton walks in the door holding a fresh-baked pie. Miss McEwing walks in a moment later wearing her best Sunday dress.

We're so glad you could join us, Mamma says.

It smells just delicious in here! Miss McEwing exclaims.

May Amelia cooked supper, Mamma says and Miss McEwing smiles at me and says, What a darling girl you are.

Maybe it was the best thing that could have happened after all because eating supper with the Jacksons has got to be the most unromantic way for a fella to court a lady. Pappa doesn't say anything and Kaarlo glares at everyone and Alvin and Ivan tease poor Isaiah and Helmi drips snot on the table and the whole time Wendell whines that everyone needs to Speak Up so he can hear what they're saying.

I ladle the stew into everyone's bowls.

What is it? Miss McEwing asks with a pleasant smile.

Fish-head stew, of course, I say. It's a Finn specialty!

Miss McEwing swallows hard and looks at her bowl.

Pappa slurps a spoonful and says, Might want to add a few more heads next time. The cheeks are what gives it the flavor.

You want some extra eyeballs? I ask her. We got plenty!

She blanches, and stammers, Uh, no thank you. I want to save some room for Mr. Clayton's lovely pie.

Wilbert and I share a secret look.

I clear away the dishes and put on the coffee and everyone goes into the parlor for dessert. I look at Mr. Clayton's pie and I'm so sad because it seems a mighty shame to waste it, but I know it will be even worse if we lose our lovely teacher. The pie is dusted on top with sugar. I will just play a little trick. I brush off the sugar and pour salt all over the top of the pie. Then I slice it up and carry it out to everyone.

Here's the pie! I say, passing out the slices.

Miss McEwing's eyes go wide when she takes her first bite.

Alvin starts choking and Ivan whacks him on the back.

Kaarlo spits his right out.

Pappa frowns and says, Eh, Jacob, a little heavy with the salt, don't you think?

Mr. Clayton takes a bite and I watch the surprise roll across his face like an ocean wave and it probably tastes just as salty, too. He looks straight in my eyes and I know he is not fooled one bit because he says, You might be right, Jalmer. Never can tell what happens in a kitchen.

But poor Miss McEwing chews and chews and chews her bite. Finally she swallows and smiles at our neighbor.

This is the best pie I've ever tasted, she declares with shining eyes, and that's when I know she is a goner for sure.

After that we must sit around in the parlor and chaperone Miss McEwing and Mr. Clayton. All Miss McEwing does is ask Question after Question of Mr. Clayton. It's like she's studying for an exam, and the subject is our neighbor.

Where did you learn to make such delicious pie? Miss McEwing asks him.

Why don't you ask him what it was like getting his fingers blown off? I suggest. That's a lot more interesting than pie.

Mamma gives an exaggerated yawn.

It certainly has been a long day. I think it's time

for Jalmer and me to head up to bed, she says, and looks at Mr. Clayton. Would you mind seeing Miss McEwing home?

It would be my pleasure, Mr. Clayton says and my teacher blushes.

You don't have to rush off yet! I say quickly. There's more pie!

May Amelia's right. Visit awhile, Mamma agrees with a wink. The children will keep you company.

But as the hour grows late and the fire dies down, the boys drift away like flies looking for sugar. First one to crawl into his bed is Kaarlo, then Ivan and Alvin, then Isaiah, until finally it's just me and Wilbert and Wendell.

Mr. Clayton's smoking a pipe and Miss McEwing has her head bent close to his to hear something he's said.

Don't fall asleep! I order Wendell and Wilbert.

I can't keep my eyes open a second longer, Wendell says, and stomps upstairs. I should've known better than to count on Wendell.

Then Wilbert stands up and starts for the stairs.

Where are you going? I hiss at my Best Brother.

To bed. They can just go ahead and get married if they want to. I can't stand another minute of it.

Well I'm staying, I say.

I stay awake as long as I can watching Mr. Clayton

and Miss McEwing, but sleep is dogging me and I can't keep my eyes open and next thing I know I'm being carried upstairs and tucked into bed next to Wilbert. I think I hear Miss McEwing's voice.

Poor dear, Miss McEwing clucks softly. She's exhausted.

Mr. Clayton chuckles. Hard work being a chaperone.

CHAPTER TEN

A Wedding to Remember

School is out and there are sunny days aplenty, and fresh berries and crawfish to fill our bellies after months of salted fish and potatoes.

On our farm we have a picnic and folks arrive by rowboat. The Norts bring their new baby girl, and everyone stands around admiring her. They've named her May Amelia after me.

Just what we need, Ivan groans. Another May Amelia.

The men talk and smoke their pipes. Old Man Weilen is there and he eyes me suspiciously.

Whose boy are you? he asks.

I ain't no boy, I say. I'm May Amelia Jackson, Mr. Weilen.

Jacksons? They just got boys, he says.

I'm a girl.

Whatcha doing in overalls then?

You think this Stanley outfit is a good invest-ment, Jalmer? Berle Holumbo's father asks Pappa.

Pappa says, *Joo.*

Mr. Petersen claps my father on the back and says, Jalmer Jackson has enough *sisu* to drive the Russians from Finland!

I remember the gold rush, Old Man Weilen says to me. I was just a boy.

Did you find any gold? I ask him.

He frowns and says, I was too late. It'd all been dug up by the time I got there.

Maybe you didn't dig in the right places, I say.

His filmy eyes focus on me in confusion. Whose Boy Are You?

There's just no talking to him, so I go into the kitchen where the women are gathered. Jane is talk-ing to Mamma. Helmi sits in the middle of the floor, rolling empty cans back and forth.

Jane looks tired and frustrated. She says, He does not know where he is anymore.

My husband was the same way, the old widow, Mrs. Paarvala says. It's hard.

This morning he didn't know who I was and thought I was trying to steal from him. He almost shot me, Jane admits.

He thinks *I'm* a boy! I say.

Mamma laughs and says, If you'd put on a dress once in a while, you'd look like a girl.

What can I do? Jane asks.

Mamma looks down at Helmi and says, Treat him like a child because that is what he is now.

The tables are groaning with all sorts of Finn treats— squeaky cheese, pickled salmon, fruit soup, and sour cream which we call *viili*. I pile my plate high with food then I go and sit between Lonny and Jaakko.

I'll bring Bosie back tomorrow, Jaakko tells me. You need him more than me.

Why? I ask.

I heard the men talking. They said your pappa will be rich soon.

Yes indeed, I say.

When you have money, people want to take it, he says darkly.

How's your kitten doing? I ask Lonny.

He wipes his arm across his face and says, A cougar ate her.

I say, My cat Buttons got burned down in the barn.

No she didn't, he says.

She did so, I say.

She's living in our shed, he insists.

My mouth drops open in disbelief. Your shed?

Yep, he says. And her kittens, too. That's why I'm not so sad about my kitten getting ate. I got a whole load of kittens to myself.

I leap up. Come on! I want to get her right now!

Buttons is curled up in a washtub hidden in the shed behind Lonny's barn. Her kittens are rolling around her. She looks up at me and blinks.

Buttons! I cry, and grab her up and give her a squeeze. I swear the fleas leap onto me, but I don't care none.

Can I keep the kittens at least? Lonny pleads.

I can't believe you've been here all along! I exclaim, and then frown at Lonny. Why didn't you tell me she wasn't dead?

I didn't know she was supposed to be dead! He narrows his eyes at me. You ain't gonna kill her, are you?

I just sigh.

The sun sinks and Wilho Saari, the best kantele player, strikes up a tune and folks start dancing.

Miss McEwing sits next to me.

This is a fine party, she declares.

Mr. Clayton walks up to us, carrying a pie.

That pie for me? I ask him.

Not exactly, he says.

Then he gets down on one knee and swallows hard.

Agnes, he says. I haven't got a ring, but I can make a pie. Will you marry me?

Miss McEwing's lips tremble and she says, Yes, Jacob, I would be delighted!

Then she throws herself into his arms. Mr. Clayton kisses my teacher soundly and every bachelor frowns.

So you're the Perfect Man, I say to Mr. Clayton.

There are no perfect men, May Amelia, he says.

I could've told him that.

Folks stay up all night dancing, and children sleep wherever they fall. In the morning everybody leaves, but Uncle Niihlo returns in the afternoon with Jaakko and Bosie.

Bosie! I cry to my scruffy little dog.

Uncle Niihlo walks up to my mother and says, Alma, it's time for me to take her back.

Right now? Mamma gasps.

I'm gonna rent out my house and we're going to live

at the logging camp, Uncle Niihlo says. They're offering free room and board. I can save more money that way.

The logging camp's dangerous for a child! Who will watch her? Mamma asks.

There's another family up there. Lady said she'd look after her for me.

Mamma looks as if she's going to burst into tears, but she bites her lip.

Helmi cries and cries until finally Jaakko walks over to his sister and kneels in front of her and whispers in her ear. She stops crying at once.

What'd you tell her? I ask him.

That we got candy back at the house. She likes sweets.

That night, Wilbert and I are back in our room. The sound of Mamma's weeping carries through the walls.

Alma, Pappa says, he's her father. It will be better for the boy. Those logging men won't look twice at that neck of his.

But she's just a little girl! my mother sobs.

I turn to Wilbert.

She wasn't hers to keep, I say.

Helmi was just like one of Buttons's kittens, Wilbert says.

You mean she had fleas?

No, May, Wilbert says. She was easy to love.

✦   ✦   ✦

Mamma hardly has time to miss little Helmi because she goes off to catch a baby and help the new mother. I think she is happy to leave us sometimes because of the loneliness of this place. Mamma says that she dreams of being able to walk out her door and talk to another woman instead of getting in a boat.

Wilbert and Isaiah and me are out in the fields checking on the sheeps. Our sheeps have no sense at all and are always getting snagged on blackberry bushes and tearing themselves up real good.

Isaiah, I say, I think this here sheep is sweet on this other one. He's always following her around.

Maybe I'll start calling them Mr. Clayton and Miss McEwing, Isaiah muses.

I think you should call them Berle and May Amelia, Wilbert says.

Humph, I say to Wilbert.

Jane is walking across the field toward us, her face worried.

Have you seen Mr. Weilen? she asks. He's been missing for a day now.

He was in the back pasture for a little while, Isaiah says. I'll go check and see if he's still there.

Jane looks relieved, and I say loudly, Isaiah, she means Mr. Weilen the Person, not Mr. Weilen the Sheep.

He reddens. Oh, sorry.

You named a sheep after my husband? Jane asks raising an eyebrow.

Least he didn't name a pig after him, Wilbert says.

Old Man Weilen turns up a few days later. He'd wandered up to the logging camp and got confused and lost his way in the woods. One of the men found him and brought him back home.

Miss McEwing and Mr. Clayton's wedding is the event of the season. Because her people live so far away, the couple get married here in Nasel at the church. Miss McEwing asks me if I will hold her bouquet during the ceremony.

Does this mean I have to wear a dress? I ask.

I'm afraid it does, she says, and even though I can think of Nothing Worse, I say Yes, because she is my favorite teacher ever.

The day of the wedding arrives and Mamma stuffs me into a scratchy dress and the boys slick back their hair and scrub their fingernails. Miss McEwing is the most beautiful bride I have ever seen. Mr. Clayton cleans up nicely, too, and he promises me that he won't help birth any calves today and ruin his nice clothes.

At the church, the preacher says, Does anybody

have any objections to these two people being married?

Every last one of us kids stands up and says, We Do.

The church goes hush-silent and Miss McEwing looks stunned and the preacher says, What exactly is your objection?

If she gets married, she can't be our teacher no more! I say. It's the rules.

Miss McEwing looks down and laughs and the preacher says, That's Not A Good Enough Reason, I'm Afraid.

But we love her, I say.

Oh May Amelia, Miss McEwing says. You'll be losing me as a teacher, but you'll be getting me as a neighbor.

It's not the same, I say.

Please sit down, all of you, the preacher orders us, which just goes to show how nobody listens to children, not even preachers.

There is a party after and instead of a wedding cake, Mr. Clayton has made a wedding pie.

Sorry about stealing your teacher away, Mr. Clayton says to me. A good wife is hard to find.

A good teacher is even harder to find, I reply.

A good husband is impossible to find, Mrs. Paarvala adds.

The party ends, and we go back to the farm, but not to bed, for we children are going to do a shivaree on Mr. Clayton and Miss McEwing. A shivaree is when you go and make a ruckus and all sorts of noise outside the newlyweds' house. We get pots and buckets and cowbells and Ivan and Alvin bring their guns. I take my favorite milking tin bucket and an enamel spoon. Mr. Clayton may have stolen our teacher, but we're gonna steal their good night's sleep.

It's a long walk in the dark and Isaiah leads the way. He is worse than any sheep for he gets us tangled in bushes and lost and finally Kaarlo takes charge.

Kaarlo says, They're gonna have babies already if we keep on following you.

We are nearly at the house when we hear a shot.

I told you not to shoot until I said so, Kaarlo says to the twins.

Wasn't us, Alvin says.

Then who was it? Kaarlo asks, and there's another shot and we hear Miss McEwing scream.

Do you think somebody is already giving them a shivaree? I ask.

Maybe Berle? Wilbert suggests.

Kaarlo says, May Amelia, go on and peek in the window to see if someone's beat us here.

Sure enough Somebody did get here before us and that Somebody is Old Man Weilen. He doesn't look like he's in a joking mood the way he's waving around his gun at poor Miss McEwing and Mr. Clayton who are in bed wearing their nightclothes. Mr. Clayton, who survived The Most Unpleasant War looks perfectly terrified.

That's My Wife! Old Man Weilen shouts, waving his gun.

Come on now, Mr. Clayton says in a soothing voice. You're just a little confused. You're just—

Old Man Weilen shoots right into the ceiling and shouts, I Ain't Confused! That's My Wife!

Miss McEwing cries, I'm Not Your Wife!

I scamper back to the boys.

Well? Kaarlo asks. Did Berle beat us here?

It ain't Berle! It's Old Man Weilen!

Old Man Weilen is doing a shivaree on Mr. Clayton and Miss McEwing? Wilbert asks.

No! He thinks Miss McEwing is his wife! He's gone crazy!

We should get Pappa, Isaiah says but there's another shot and Miss McEwing screams and I say, We Got To Save Them!

But what do we do? Wilbert asks.

Kaarlo looks at me and smiles and says, I have a plan.

*   *   *

Kaarlo's Plan is for me to distract Old Man Weilen so that he and the twins can get through the window and knock him down, which I don't think is much of a plan but nobody asked my opinion. As I walk through the front door of Mr. Clayton's house, I can't help but wonder if the Real Plan is to Get Rid Of Me because Old Man Weilen looks more ornery than Friendly.

May Amelia! Miss McEwing gasps.

Hiya, Miss McEwing, I say. Hiya, Mr. Clayton.

Mr. Clayton shouts, Get Out Of Here! But it's too late and Old Man Weilen whirls on me.

Hiya, Mr. Weilen.

Whose boy are you? he asks.

I ain't no boy, I say. I'm May Amelia Jackson.

Jacksons? They just got boys, he says.

No, sir, I say. They got me, too.

What are you doing here? he asks belligerently, and behind him I see Kaarlo's face in the window.

What are *you* doing here? I ask him.

He cocks his head at me, and his face is full of confusion like he is a lost child.

I, he says, his lower lip trembling, I—

Behind him Kaarlo is raising the milking bucket and is about to bring it right down on the old fella's head when I say, You came for pie?

127

Old Man Weilen blinks and says, That's right. I came for pie.

Kaarlo hesitates, and I say to Old Man Weilen, Come on out to the kitchen, and the old man drops his gun and follows me like a docile lamb.

I sit him down and give him a piece of pie which he eats happily.

Oh May Amelia! Miss McEwing says. You were so brave!

Mr. Clayton gives a low whistle and says, Brave? That was a foolish thing you did, May Amelia.

Wasn't my idea, I say.

Old Man Weilen pauses midbite and looks at me. Whose boy are you?

I sigh.

I'm Jalmer Jackson's boy, I say.

CHAPTER ELEVEN

The Right Hand

All the Finnish ladies like to keep a clean house and Mamma is no exception. Pappa says that the spiders don't stand a chance against my mother's broom.

We have been cleaning all day long—sweeping and scrubbing pots with hemlock branches. Mamma is cleaning the stove with a fresh seagull wing from the bird Ivan shot for her for that morning. She swears it's the best way to clean the stove, but I still feel sorry for the poor seagull.

I polish the floor with skim milk to make it shine.

Not much point if you ask me, I say to Mamma.

It'll just get dirty right quick again with all the boys and their boots.

You may be right, May Amelia, she says.

Mamma, I say, when we are rich, we can hire a girl to clean the house.

She straightens, rubbing her back. No one will clean your house as well as you. How was Jane when you saw her?

I took fresh-baked bread and some of Mamma's blackberry preserves to Jane earlier this morning. Old Man Weilen's mind never returned after the night of the shivaree, and so Jane had to send him to the hospital in Astoria. He escaped a week later and got killed when a wagon ran him over. Poor Jane is a widow now. It feels strange not to see the old man sitting on the porch asking me whose boy I am.

She's sad, I say. She misses him bad.

It was a blessing, Mamma says. Believe me, there are worse things than dying, May Amelia.

Alvin bursts in the door, his muddy feet tracking across all my hard work.

Alvin! I shout at him. You're making a mess!

Ivan's hurt! he shouts, and that's when I notice the blood on his overalls, like he just got finished slaughtering chickens, and I know something bad has happened.

Mamma grabs her birthing bag and says May

Amelia, Fetch As Many Cobwebs As You Can.

Everyone knows that cobwebs are good at stopping bleeding. I go running to the shed since there's no chance of there being a web in the house after us cleaning.

By the time we get to the camp, they've got Ivan laid out on one of the wooden tables where the men eat, and Uncle Niihlo is holding his hand and saying It'll Be Okay, Son. Ivan's hand is wrapped in a bloody flour sack and his leg is propped at an angle that no leg should be. He is moaning with pain.

What happened? Mamma demands.

He fell between two logs and got smashed up good, Uncle Niihlo says. I'm so sorry, Alma.

Let me see his hand, Mamma orders in the no-nonsense voice she uses on birthing mothers.

The kind cook who bandaged my leg unwraps the bloody fabric and Mamma gasps, because it's plain as day that all the cobwebs in the world aren't gonna save my brother's hand. It's been ground to bits and barely looks like a hand at all.

Ivan shrieks in pain, and Mamma drops her bag and walks out of the hall. I run after her.

Where are you going, Mamma?

I Cannot Bear To Bury Another Child, she says, every word clear. My mother walks into the thick woods, and she never looks back.

The men get Ivan down the mountain and Uncle Aarno and Pappa take him to Astoria, where the doctor sets his leg. But they can do nothing for his hand and they must chop it off or it will rot and then Ivan will die. Alvin stays by his twin's side the entire time.

When Ivan finally comes home, he's thin and pale and there's just a stump of bandages where his right hand used to be. He is a different boy. He cannot even be bothered to be mean to me anymore and I almost miss it, for the new Ivan is weird and lost. Everything is hard for him and I hear him sob when he tries to pick up his gun with his one good hand. At meals he must rely on his twin to cut up his food. Alvin trails after him everywhere like a worried mother hen.

Isaiah, who is clever, takes a glove and stuffs it with batting so that when it's tied onto the end of Ivan's stump, it looks like a hand. But it doesn't work like one.

At suppertime, Wendell says, Can you pass the potatoes, Ivan?

Alvin reaches out to grab the bowl of potatoes, but Ivan bangs the table with his stump and snaps, He asked *me* to pass him the potatoes!

We all watch as Ivan struggles to pick up the bowl with his good left hand and the glove stump, but it goes clattering to the floor, boiled potatoes rolling everywhere. Ivan tears off the glove and throws it across the room.

I Want My Hand Back! Ivan howls, and Alvin flinches.

Pappa tries to soothe Ivan by telling him that when we are rich he will buy him a carved hand, the finest one ever, so that nobody knows the difference.

I don't want a carved hand! I want My Hand!

You can't have it back! Pappa snaps.

But it's in that hospital! It's there! Part of me is there and I want it back!

You want your hand back? The part that was sawed off? Kaarlo asks.

I want to give it a proper burial! Ivan says, and there is a crazed look in his eyes, and he reminds me of poor old Mr. Weilen.

Later that night, Ivan wakes up the whole house. He is smashing the kitchen to bits, just tossing cups and plates and jars and muttering about how He Wants His Hand Back Now. And for a boy who just lost a hand he's got a lot of fight in him. It takes Alvin, Kaarlo, and Pappa to stop him and finally they just lock him in Mr. Petersen's sauna for the rest of the night with Alvin standing guard.

Kaarlo's pale the next morning and much as he was jealous of Ivan getting to work at the logging camp, I can tell he wouldn't wish this on anyone.

He's gone plumb crazy, Kaarlo says.

Alvin looks even worse. He says, We got to get that hand back somehow.

Pappa nods.

Pappa gives me the instructions. Wilbert and I are to go to the hospital in Astoria and ask for Ivan's hand and bring it back home. Uncle Aarno will take us over, but we are to tell no one what we are doing.

What if they don't have it anymore? Wilbert asks.

Just ask them to give you *any hand*, Pappa says in exasperation.

As we sail across the Columbia, I look at Wilbert, and say, They got hands just lying around in hospitals?

Guess so. They probably got ears, too. Maybe even toes.

When we show up at the hospital there's a lady at the desk.

'Scuse me, I say. We come for my brother's hand. Ivan Jackson.

The lady gives me a long strange look and then walks out and then comes back with a man who looks like a doctor.

Is there something I can help you children with? he asks.

We need to get our brother's hand back, I say.

What do you need his hand for? the doctor asks.

'Cause he's gone crazy and he wants it back to give it a proper burial so Pappa sent us to fetch it, I say.

The doctor rubs his nose and says, That hand is long gone, I'm afraid. There wasn't much left of it.

But you don't understand. We really need a hand! I whisper, It don't have to be the Exact Hand. Just got to be a Right Hand.

I'm very sorry, the doctor says. But we can't help you.

Me and Wilbert go outside and watch the ships come in.

What do we do now? Wilbert asks.

Otto will know what to do, I say. He knows Everything about Astoria.

We go to the cannery where Otto's mom works and Otto is there. He is delivering lunch to the men.

Hiya, Otto! I say.

What are you doing here? Otto asks.

We need your help, I say.

For what?

I guess you could say that We Could Really Use A Hand.

I explain to Otto everything that has happened with poor Ivan and my friend just nods and says, I think I know who can help us: the Widow Mariah.

So off we go running to Mariah's Tavern, where lunch is over and men are walking in and drinking their wages away. Mariah is in the kitchen.

You're too early for the fritters, she says when she sees us. I haven't put them in for supper yet and those men cleaned me out at lunch.

You got any dead bodies lying around? Otto asks.

Mariah doesn't look the least bit surprised to be asked such a thing. I guess when you're in the shanghaiing business, nothing surprises you.

You planning on being a doctor? she drawls.

My brother Ivan lost his hand and he wants it back, I say.

We went to the hospital but they'd already thrown it away and they didn't have any spares, Wilbert says.

Ivan's gone crazy, I say. Pappa says not to come home without a hand.

Mariah gives us a long slow look and tosses her braid over her shoulder.

I've had stranger requests, she says. Let me see what I can do.

I always knew Astoria was a wonderful wicked place, what with all the exciting things happening, but who knew a body could just waltz in and get a hand if you knew the right person? Mariah gives us a potato sack and inside is a hand.

Whose is it? Wilbert asks her.

You don't want to know, she says. Believe me.

The whole way back to Nasel we peek in the bag to look at The Hand.

It looks too good, Wilbert says. He's going to know it's not his.

So when we get off the boat we take The Hand and bang it up and smash it on a few trees.

That's more like it, I say.

Wilbert gives me a funny look. You think the hand will miss being with the rest of its body?

I don't know about that, but I do know that I've never seen my brother Ivan look as happy as when we give him that potato sack. It's like we've given him a bag of gold.

He smiles and says, I want to bury it in the back pasture.

And that's what we do. Isaiah builds a little box for it and Mamma convinces the preacher to come and when it's all over, there's a dead body somewhere across the Columbia that's missing a hand, but we've got our brother back.

After that, whenever we hear the tree scratching against the house in the dark of night, I whisper to Wilbert, That's Ivan's Hand Trying To Get Back To Its Body In Astoria.

CHAPTER TWELVE

Our Loving Family

Hay making is the most bone-tiring time on the farm and every Jackson child must help. We make hay while the sun shines, for if the hay is too wet, it's No Good and it can burn down your barn which is what happened to the Teppolas two summers ago. Not that we have a barn to worry about right now. Pappa says we will build a new one when we get the Stanley money. In the meantime, Mr. Clayton says we can store our hay in his barn.

We gather the hay into piles we call shocks and then Kaarlo drives the wagon along and we put the hay in it. It's been hot all week and we take a dip in the Nasel every chance we can get, which is not very often because our brother Kaarlo has turned into a tyrant.

You Are Slower Than Molasses! he shouts to try and make us work faster, but Wendell can't hear him and I just ignore him.

He's practicing at being Pappa, I say to Wilbert.

Wilbert grimaces. He don't need to practice. He's already good at it.

I hear a bell ringing and there is a boat coming down the Nasel toward our little dock.

It's Uncle Aarno! I cry, and take off toward the boat.

Kaarlo shouts after me, May Amelia Jackson You Come Back Here Right Now! but I can't be bothered by bossy brothers, not when my favorite uncle is visiting.

Uncle Aarno slows the boat down by the dock and tosses me a rope to tie it off.

Hiya, Uncle Aarno, I call.

Got some mail for you sweetheart, he says, and hands me a small packet of letters.

Think up any new ways to die? I ask him.

I'd say there is a pretty good chance your father might shoot me, he says in a wry voice.

Why would he do that?

Because he helped me, a familiar voice says and there is my handsome oldest brother, Matti, grinning in the cabin doorway with a girl next to him. It must be Mary O'Casey, but my eyes can't get past her big belly to look at her face. Matti is taller than ever and he's wearing nice clothes, store-boughten from the looks of them, and Mary's got on a real fine dress, not gunnysack like Mamma's.

Aren't you going to say anything, May Amelia? Matti finally asks.

Pappa's gonna kill You, I say.

He laughs.

Honest, I say. You show up and there are shot-guns lying around and there's no telling what's gonna happen!

It'll be fine, Matti says. How've you been, May Amelia?

Baby Amy died, I say.

I know, May Amelia. Auntie Alice wrote me. She said you took it very hard. I'm sorry I wasn't here for you.

And maybe because he's my big brother Matti, the one I've always been able to count on, it seems all right to say what's in my heart.

It was terrible, I whisper. The most terrible thing ever.

Oh my little May, he says, and I just throw myself

into his arms before the tears hit my cheeks. I bury my face in his strong warm chest.

I've missed you so, Matti, I say, my voice muffled.

I missed you, too, my only May Amelia, he says.

Uncle Aarno insists on walking with us to the house.

Just In Case, he says and I say, Just In Case You Gotta Bury Matti?

I never did know Mary O'Casey very well but she seems sweet and kind with her apple cheeks and brown eyes and thick black hair pinned back under her fancy hat. And then of course there's her belly, which is like a firm little sack of potatoes.

There was a real good turnout, I tell her. Everybody brought plenty of food.

For what? she asks.

Your funeral, of course. Everyone thought you drowned in the river.

Her face turns white.

They looked for your body for days. And your mamma cried and cried. She fainted too.

Matti! Mary says anxiously. What are we going to do?

He puts an arm around her waist, and smiles. Everything'll be fine, Mary. You'll see.

You've forgotten what Pappa's like, I say.

Matti straightens his back and turns to Mary and says, You wait outside for a moment until I fetch you.

I can tell that she is only too happy to put off greeting her new family.

The boys have come in from the fields and are sitting at the kitchen table drinking coffee with Pappa. Mamma's making a pie crust, rolling out the dough with a pin.

Uncle Aarno clears his throat loudly and says, I brought you something from Astoria.

Matti steps through the door and Mamma's rolling pin goes clattering to the floor.

Mamma! Matti says, crossing to her side and grabbing her before she tumbles over.

Oh, Matti, she says, and bursts into tears and clutches him to her.

The rest of the boys are frozen in place, unsure what to do. Everyone's waiting to see what Pappa will say.

Pappa, Matti says.

Pappa's staring at Matti like he's seeing a ghost.

Matti? he says, his throat thick. Is it really you, son?

Yes, Pappa, Matti says.

Matti! Pappa says, and is across the room in two steps embracing Matti.

All we can do is stare as Pappa pats Matti on the back, tears running down his cheeks.

Pappa lets Matti loose and says, Let me look at you, son. Did they hurt you?

I'm fine, Pappa, Matti says with a little laugh.

Where'd those shanghaiers take you? Pappa asks. China? Japan?

That's the thing, Pappa, Matti says clearing his throat. I wasn't shanghaied. Not exactly.

Pappa frowns. Not shanghaied?

Matti raises a finger and opens the door and says, Come in, sweetheart.

Mary O'Casey, or I reckon she's Mary Jackson now, steps into the kitchen.

Hello, Mr. Jackson, Mary says.

Pappa blanches.

Ain't you supposed to be dead? Wendell asks Mary.

She looks real alive to me, Kaarlo says sarcastically.

Matti puts his arm around Mary and says, We got married.

Married? Pappa growls, and I can hear the storm coming but before the first lightning strikes, Matti says, You're gonna be a grandfather, Pappa.

Grandfather?

Mary's expecting, Matti explains, rubbing Mary's belly.

We hadn't noticed, Kaarlo says.

The cows are lowing outside and I think these are going to be the last sounds I hear before Pappa kills Matti. Instead, Pappa just sighs, and says I Sure Do Hope It's A Boy.

The boys pester Matti with questions about San Francisco and Mamma pesters Mary with questions about how she's feeling. The only one who doesn't say a word is Kaarlo. He just stares at Matti through sullen eyes.

What happened to your hand, Ivan? Matti asks in shock.

Ivan just waves his stump and says, Oh, it's in the back pasture.

Tell us about your job, Matti, Pappa says.

It's real good money, Pappa, Matti says. I've already worked up to being manager for unloading the boats.

Pappa says, Humph, but I can tell he's pleased.

I'm thinking of starting my own unloading business for boats coming from Finland and Sweden, Matti adds. The men trust me.

Maybe I can help you with that, Pappa says, and then tells Matti about investing in the Stanley Company.

How about that, Matti says, sitting back. Little old Nasel a port city?

We're gonna be rich, Matti! I say.

How long will you be in town? Pappa asks.

Least a week, Matti says.

Pappa nods. Plenty of time to talk about this. I'm real proud of you, Matti.

Kaarlo grimaces and says, I got to check on the cows, and bangs back his chair and is out the door before anyone says anything.

Mamma can't stop smiling. She keeps saying that her whole loving family is back under one roof. And Matti and Pappa spend every waking moment together. They walk around the farm, heads bent talking about starting businesses. I haven't seen Pappa so happy in a long time and he even takes Matti to the sauna on Saturday night.

It's like the King himself has returned, Kaarlo grumbles.

But it's Matti, I say.

Matti! Matti! I'm sick of it!

You're just jealous.

Jealous? he scoffs.

Truth is, I reckon we're all a little bit jealous of Matti, even me. Pappa has never paid much mind to any of the other boys. It's always been Matti for as long as I can remember and it would bother me except I love Matti so very much. Still I am starting to see Kaarlo with different eyes. He works hard day in and day out and yet it is Matti who gets kind words and praise.

But if all the boys are jealous of Matti, every last one of them is a little in love with Mary. She is cheerful and helps Mamma and me in the kitchen. The boys don't tussle as much with her around and they're a lot cleaner for some reason. Maybe having a pretty girl in a house makes boys behave better.

Matti and Mary visited her parents right after they came to our house. Her folks were overjoyed to learn she wasn't dead, but they weren't overjoyed about Matti.

Are your folks mad at you? I ask my new sister-in-law.

Very, Mary says. But they're happy about the baby.

Are *you* happy about that baby?

I didn't think it would happen so fast, she admits.

I'm not surprised, I say.

Why? she asks.

Because Mamma always says that Babies and Bad News come when they're least expected.

There is still hay to be brought in, so every child gets back to work, including Matti, because he is a Jackson boy.

We are out in the fields pitching the hay into the back of the wagon.

Matti touches the hay with his hand and says, It's too wet. Let it lie.

Kaarlo says, It's dry enough.

I'm telling you, it's not, Matti says.

Don't you tell me what to do, Kaarlo snarls.

What's the matter with you? Matti asks, confusion plain on his face.

You ain't in charge no more.

What? Matti says, and this seems to enrage Kaarlo.

When you left, you lost your right to tell anyone else what to do! Kaarlo shouts. Do you know how hard we've had to work? Poor Ivan here lost his hand because we needed more money and all you can talk about is how Wonderful your life is. Well, our life hasn't been wonderful. It's been downright Hard, and I'm not gonna listen to you telling me what to do when I've been the one bleeding for this farm.

The boys and me just stare at Kaarlo. I don't think I've ever heard him talk this much in my whole life.

Matti says, You ain't even a real Jackson.

Kaarlo flings down his pitchfork.

Make Hay King Matti, he snorts, and stomps off.

How could you say that, Matti? I ask him.

My big brother looks a little ashamed. Sorry, May Amelia. I'll find him and apologize.

* * *

The night before Matti and Mary return to San Francisco, Mary's parents throw a party at their house to celebrate their daughter's marriage to Matti. Kaarlo refuses to come.

There will be lots of good food, I tell him, but he says, I'd rather clean the outhouse than go there.

Folks shower the happy couple with presents. Pappa uses the last of the money from Mr. Yerrington to buy a grand wedding gift for the new couple—a new suit for Matti.

You got to look right for business, Pappa says.

Thanks, Pappa, Matti says.

I'm making a cradle for the babe, Pappa tells Mary, and she blushes prettily.

The next morning, Uncle Aarno comes and fetches Matti and Mary in his boat. Matti hugs everyone goodbye except for Kaarlo, who's nowhere to be found.

May Amelia, Matti says to me. If you ever need me, all you have to do is write and I'll come home. I promise.

I know, Matti, I say.

When I get back to the house, I find Kaarlo sitting at the kitchen table drinking coffee.

He's gone, I tell him.

Good riddance, Kaarlo says.

CHAPTER THIRTEEN

I Take My Lumps

It is September, and the evenings are cool. Supper's over and the dishes are washed. We are setting in the parlor in front of the fire. Mamma is piecing together a quilt and I am knitting socks. Pappa is standing by the mantel fingering his lump of lead. There is a real smile on his face. I think it's maybe only the second time I've ever seen him smile. He is smiling because he received a letter from Mr. Yerrington saying that we will be able to cash in the stock sometime after Christmas.

The lead was right after all, Pappa says, looking at Mamma. Our ship has finally sailed.

Oh, Jalmer, Mamma says.

In the distance, there is a loud shot. A cougar got another one of our sheeps, so Wild Cat Clark is out hunting for him right now.

Kaarlo says, Pappa, have you given any thought to my idea of opening an oyster cannery in Astoria?

There's enough canneries already, Pappa says. I'm going to move the family to San Francisco as soon as we get the money.

San Francisco? Isaiah gasps. But what about the sheeps?

So we can be near Matti? I ask.

Pappa nods and says, He has some good ideas for businesses to invest in there.

Kaarlo looks like he would spit in Pappa's face if he had the *sisu*.

Pappa picks up my lump of lead and says, Your fortune was right after all, May Amelia.

What do you mean? I ask.

Your lump meant you would have Good Ears this year. We couldn't have made the deal with Mr. Yerrington without you doing the translating for me.

I have Good Ears? Wendell asks.

Not You, Wilbert says loudly. May Amelia.

And then Pappa says the words I never thought

I would hear cross his lips. He says, You Did Good, Girl.

Mamma smiles at me, and my heart just about bursts out of my overalls.

Ivan asks, Did my lump predict my hand getting chopped off?

No one says anything to that.

There's a knock at the door, and I open it expecting to see Wild Cat Clark standing there with a cougar flung over his shoulder. But instead of the famous hunter, it's Lonny, and there are tears running down his cheeks.

Daddy shot himself, he says just as matter-of-factly as if he was saying he milked the cows.

What did you say, son? Pappa asks.

Daddy went into the barn and shot himself. Can I have supper here tonight?

Merciful heavens, Mamma says, and everyone jumps up at once and goes running out the door. I start to follow, but Mamma shouts, Stay with Lonny, May Amelia!

Then it's just me and Lonny.

You okay, Lonny? I ask.

I don't think so, he says.

You want something to eat? I ask, and he says, Daddy forgot to make supper today. And lunch and breakfast.

Come on, I say.

We go into the kitchen and I spoon out some *laksloda* onto a plate. I set it in front of him and he starts to eat.

This tastes good, he says. Then he lays his face down on the table and starts crying.

Turns out that the only lead that predicted the future was the bullet from Mr. Petersen's gun. Now we know why Mr. Petersen is dead and poor Lonny an orphan. There is no Stanley Company. There is no stock. Mr. Yerrington was a fake. He took our money and has disappeared.

We have lost everything.

Mr. Petersen discovered the news because he has a cousin who is a clerk in a bank in San Francisco. Pappa found the letter next to Mr. Petersen's body.

The funeral for Mr. Petersen is sad. Everyone comes out for it and Lonny wanders off halfway through the service, saying he doesn't want to see his daddy put in the ground. Folks cry and cry. Wilbert says that the people crying the most are the ones who invested in Stanley.

Lonny moves in with us because he has no kin left. It isn't much different having him around, since he was already eating here most nights anyways. The preacher says we are charitable to take him in, but that is the only kind thing anybody says to us. The Stanley scheme has swept through the valley like a storm. At first folks were so shocked they didn't know what to do, but now they are angry and everyone is blaming Jalmer Jackson for their Misfortune.

The church is quiet when we Jacksons walk in, and people give us angry looks. Pappa refuses to come with us because he cannot bear to see the faces of the other men who invested in the scheme on his word. I have heard that the Petersens, and the Niemis, and the Paarlas, are all ruined, for they mortgaged their farms heavily and now they cannot make the payments. No one has seen or heard from Mr. Yerrington. If I hadn't met him myself, I would've thought he was just something I dreamed up.

But the worst shock of all is finding out that Mr. Clayton *hasn't* lost his farm. He hasn't lost it because he never invested.

I didn't trust that Yerrington fella, I overhear Mr. Clayton tell Pappa. He had a touch of the snake oil-man about him.

And I have never been so unhappy at someone else's good fortune. For I was so sure that Mr. Yerrington said that Mr. Clayton was going in with the Stanley Company.

What if I translated something else Mr. Yerrington said wrong? I ask Wilbert.

It wouldn't be your fault, Wilbert assures me. He probably just lied to you.

But all I can think about is the cannery where Otto's mother works. Because I feel just like some poor salmon on the table waiting for a knife to chop off its head.

Nobody talks about the future now, or about living in San Francisco and opening businesses. No one talks about anything. It's as if a child has died, a child that never even had a chance to live, except maybe in our dreams, and like Mamma always says, there is nothing worse than thinking of a baby that did not get born.

Pappa is full of righteous fury and decides he will fight This Injustice. He has me write letters to Important Persons who he thinks will help us. He says that he is an Honest Man and deserves to be dealt with fairly. He dictates to me.

Dear Mr. President McKinley, he says. I am a citizen of the United States residing in Washington, Pacific County. My family has recently suffered the most inhuman treatment at the hands of a well-organized lawless body of tyrannical thieves under the leadership of a man going by the name of F. B. Yerrington, formerly of Carson City, Nevada. This man—

Can you go a little slower please, Pappa? I ask. I can't write that fast.

Pappa sends letter after letter after letter. To the president. To the governor. To the senator. But the president does not write back, and neither do the governor, or the senator. I hope it's not because I have bad penmanship and spelled words wrong. I hope it's because they are big men who are too busy for the little problems of the Jacksons.

The sound of Mamma and Pappa fighting wakes me up.

How are we going to pay the mortgage, Jalmer? Mamma demands.

We can sell some of the cows, Pappa says in a weary voice.

We'd have to sell every last one of them to pay the bank! she wails.

Well, what do you want me to do? he shouts, and my mother starts sobbing.

A few days later, Pappa auctions off all our cows. Even Patience.

We have a new teacher at the schoolhouse and his name is Mr. Trebble. He is a sour man who doesn't let us learn our lessons in our underdrawers and punishes us if we talk Finn.

Speak English or there will be Trouble, Mr. Trebble says, rapping his ruler against the desk.

Poor Charles gets the worst of it because he has such a hard time with the English. He ends up getting his knuckles rapped so much that they are bright red.

The boys start calling him Mr. Trouble behind his back. And Mr. Trebble doesn't have a high opinion of Girls in general, and Me in particular.

Waste of schooling if you ask me, he says. You'll just have babies someday.

But Mr. Trebble is not the only one giving me a hard time. At lunchtime, no one wants to play with us Jackson children.

Nuutti comes up to where Wilbert and I are sitting and says, My daddy says that we're gonna lose our farm and it's all because of the Jacksons.

Wilbert stares stonily at the ground.

My mother's been crying every night! Nuutti says.

I try and close my ears, but I can't. For once, I wish I was deaf as Wendell.

We're gonna get turned out of our own house and it's your daddy's fault!

Wilbert's fist clenches and I say, Don't Pay Him Any Mind, Wilbert.

But Nuutti is like Friendly the Bull and he doesn't stop, he just keeps on chasing you.

My daddy says your daddy should be ashamed of tricking so many people. He says your daddy was in on the scheme, he says—

I never find out whatever else Nuutti's dad says because Wilbert hauls off and hits him.

The teacher punishes Wilbert by rapping him on the knuckles with his ruler, but the truth is no amount of rapping can make up for the punishment we Jackson children are going through.

On Saturday night, the men do not take a sauna because Mr. Petersen is dead and it was his sauna. Instead they all go drinking. I keep Mamma company as she waits up for Pappa. We card wool for socks, but Mamma's face is pinched. I know she is worried.

I bet Uncle Aarno would lend us money if we asked him, I say.

Your father would rather die than take money from his brother.

But why? I don't understand.

She looks down. A man's pride is a terrible thing, May Amelia.

There's a knock at the door and Mamma opens it and there is Mr. Clayton with Pappa slumped against him. He's got a bloody nose and looks dead to the world.

Sorry, Alma, Mr. Clayton says.

What happened? Mamma asks in a tired voice.

Someone else started it, Mr. Clayton says.

Looks like Someone Else finished it, too, Mamma says.

Pappa does not give up hope that this Wrong will be Righted. He does not give up hope when Mamma cries late at night. He does not give up hope until the letter arrives from the bank telling us that we must vacate the farm because we haven't paid the mortgage.

My father goes to see the bank to plead our case, but when he returns, he walks straight to the fireplace. He flings the stock certificates into the fire and watches them burn. Then he takes to his chair and he does not get up. For a whole day, he just sits there, not saying a word to anyone, not even to Mamma. He just stares into the fire. He is still there the next morning when we come in for breakfast after we've finished our chores.

Mamma says to me, I'm worried about your father. Bring him his breakfast.

I walk into the parlor, and say, Pappa, here's breakfast.

He looks at me and his eyes are burning. He's fingering the lumps of melted lead.

This is all your fault, he says in a low voice.

Pappa?

You've Ruined Us, Girl! he says, every word a curse.

He flings the lumps of lead at me and I stumble back, dropping the bowl of porridge. It spills everywhere.

You're the one that translated what that man said! he shouts, and it stings worse than if he'd struck me, because it's true.

But Pappa—

You're the one who read the papers!

Please, Pappa—

You Are the Reason We Have Lost Everything! You! You Useless Girl! he roars.

And then his shoulders slump like the fight has gone out of him and he starts sobbing, a broken man, and I turn around and all the boys and Mamma are standing there, shocked looks on their faces, but no one defends me, no one says a word, and I look at Wilbert, my Best Brother, and he won't meet my eyes.

Wilbert, I whisper.

But he doesn't say anything, and something inside of me curls up and dies.

Then Ivan says, If we have to leave the farm, I'm digging up my hand and taking it.

*   *   *

I don't think. I just run to the Nasel and take the rowboat and go to the Baby Island. I hide myself and my shame in the sorcerer's tree because it is the only place I can think of where I won't have to see the disappointed looks on my family's faces at discovering what must surely be the truth. It's All My Fault.

Darkness falls and I wait and wait and wait for Wilbert to come and find me like he always does, but my brother Wilbert does not come. No one comes but the wind and the rain and the thick feeling that this will never be better, that I will never be forgiven.

I am in Trouble Forever.

CHAPTER FOURTEEN

What Ghosts Want

It's as if I've died but I am still here, like one of the
Finn ghosts haunting the tidelands. Pappa refuses to
speak to me and the boys follow his lead, and I don't
know if it's because they agree with him, or because
they're scared of him. I don't know which is worse.

This isn't like washing out the yeast starter,
Wilbert says.

Lonny's the only one who talks to me, but that's
just because he doesn't know any better. He doesn't
know that I am the reason for his poor father's death.
That I, May Amelia Jackson, a Useless Girl, am to

blame for the terrible Misfortune that has befallen the whole of Nasel.

I can hardly bear to go to the schoolhouse but I do because it means I can get away from the farm and Pappa. But even the schoolhouse does not give me any relief, for every day there is another empty desk, another family disappeared into the night because they have lost all their money in the Stanley scheme. First to go is Nuutti, and next is Waino, and then, finally, Berle.

Where's Berle? I ask.

They moved away. I hear his daddy is looking for work in the cranberry bogs, Charles says.

The sight of Berle's empty desk is more painful than Pappa's condemning eyes, and when Mr. Trebble asks why I am crying, I say that I feel sick. Because I do.

I write to Matti telling him what has happened and that we need his help. I know my big brother will come home as soon as he gets word. But the only person who comes is Uncle Aarno, and he brings a letter from the new owner of our farm that says the sheriff will turn us out if we do not vacate the premises. Uncle Aarno and Pappa and Mamma sit around the kitchen table, talking.

I'll fight it, Pappa says. To my dying breath.

You got to face facts, Jalmer, Uncle Aarno urges.

Where will we go, Jalmer? Mamma says, sounding like she is going to cry. What will we do? How will we feed all these children?

Uncle Aarno says, Rent Niihlo's place. He hasn't found anyone yet. It's small, but it's got lots of land. Needs to be cleared, of course, but you can farm it. Maybe even buy it from Niihlo someday?

This Is My Farm, Pappa says punctuating each word with his fist on the table. I proved up every inch of this land!

You got to think about the future, Jalmer, Uncle Aarno says.

We wouldn't be in this situation if it weren't for Her, he says glaring at me.

Jalmer! Uncle Aarno snaps. It isn't May Amelia's fault. You weren't the only one taken in by this Yerrington fellow. Folks all over town believed him.

They went in because *I* went in, Pappa insists, and his eyes fix on me. And *I* went in because of *her*.

You're being ridiculous. She's a good girl, Uncle Aarno says. If you were thinking straight, you wouldn't say such a thing.

You can have her, Pappa says. She's Not My Daughter Anymore.

The world tilts, and Mamma cries, Jalmer!

You're meaner than Mother was, Uncle Aarno says. Then he stands up and says in a gentle voice,

Pack your things, May Amelia. You're coming with me.

No one says good-bye.

Not even Wilbert.

Uncle Aarno's wife has been dead these many years, so he knows how to cook and clean and take care of himself. He can mend all sorts of things—socks, fishing nets, even a broken clock. I wish he could mend my father's heart but I don't think anyone can do that. My uncle says I must forgive my father for being a bitter man, that it isn't his fault, that their mother made him hard and unkind by never showing a speck of love. He says that this is just a storm, and all storms blow over. That may be, but even I know that sailors drown sometimes.

Here in Uncle Aarno's house I can almost pretend that I never had a family—a herd of boys, a mamma so sweet that other children wished she was theirs, and a pappa fierce enough to scare bears away with his eyebrows. I finally have my own bed in my own room and I don't have to fight for the covers or listen to snores, but I can't sleep. All I can think about is Old Man Weilen. Every last person said it was such a shame that he lost his mind, that he couldn't remember what he ate for breakfast or who his wife was, but I know different. He was Lucky. I would give anything to forget the loathing in Pappa's eyes and the disappointment in Wilbert's and the hopelessness in Mamma's. I wish I could forget it all, but I can't. It's as clear as rainwater.

I help Uncle Aarno deliver the mail and learn all sorts of things. People tell him everything. Briita Salme hates her daughter-in-law and thinks her son could have done better. Gussie Mattson's cousin made it to New York City on a boat but he was coughing so much when he arrived that they wouldn't let him in, and he had to go all the way back to Finland.

When a letter arrives addressed to Jaakko, I can't help myself; I open it and read it. I guess I'm just as nosy as every other Finn. The letter has no return address and all that's inside is a newspaper clipping from Finland. It reports that a man named Martti Larson has been sentenced to life imprisonment for the murder of Jaakko's mother. I hope my cousin will finally be able to sleep at night.

I wait and wait for one of my brothers to sneak away and visit me at Uncle Aarno's, but it is the women who end up coming. I guess they're better at forgiving than men. They probably have to be to do the washing every week.

Mamma is the first one to come and I'm so shocked to see her that the words get stuck in my throat and I feel like Buttons trying to cough up a hairball. Nothing comes out.

Your father doesn't know I'm here, she admits. I told him I was catching a baby.

I say, Mamma I'm So Sorry! and start crying.

She just hugs me and says, Oh, My Little May.

We visit for a while on the porch and she tells me that Pappa is still dictating letters to the president and everyone else he can think of. She says poor Wendell's hand has near about fallen off from all the writing.

I miss the boys, I say.

She looks away and sighs. You have to give your father some time. He'll come round.

Then she says, I came to tell you that I've taken a job at a cannery in Astoria. A cannery? I whisper.

I dearly love catching babies, she says, but nobody pays me. We need the money and I can stay with Aunt Alice.

Jane is the next lady to visit and she brings her kind smile and a basket. When she opens it, out tumbles Buttons my cat.

Oh Buttons! I cry, and I am so happy to see my flea-bitten cat. Buttons just purrs against me and I know she is happy to see me, too.

Jane says, Your brother Wilbert thought you might be missing her.

Uncle Aarno invites Jane to stay for supper and he tells tales to amuse us. Like about the time he was out gillnetting and got stuck in a bad storm. It took him a day to tack back and everybody thought he was dead.

By the time I made it home, my wife had had three proposals of marriage! he tells us.

Jane gives a knowing chuckle, and says, Three? I have had fifteen proposals since my husband died.

We stay up late into the night talking and no one mentions my family losing the farm and how I am to blame and how I have ruined everything. For one night I am happy as an old man who has lost his mind because I Forget.

I beg Uncle Aarno to take me out gillnetting with him.

It's dangerous work, he says.

Not any more dangerous than school, I say. At least Friendly can't get me out on the river.

True enough, he agrees.

We go out at night because high tide is the best time to put in the nets. Most of the gillnetters don't own their own boats and work for the packing companies, but Uncle Aarno used the money that Grandmother Patience left him to buy his. He has a mate, a young Finn man fresh from Kaustinen named Tuuni, who is full of energy. I help the men set the nets in and then we drift waiting for the silly salmon to swim into them and get caught on their gills.

The boat bobs on the water in the darkness. We eat our dinner and watch the stars. I pretend that Wilbert is looking at the same stars as me.

Soon it is time to start hauling in our catch. It is hard work indeed for the nets are heavy and long. Uncle Aarno tells me his are two hundred feet. By morning, our boat is full of salmon and I am plumb exhausted.

Tuuni says in an admiring voice, May Amelia, you'd make a good gillnetter. You work harder than any boy I've met.

That's 'cause I'm a girl, I say.

Uncle Aarno takes me with him to Astoria when he goes to fetch the mail, so that I can visit Mamma at the cannery. As we sail over, I think of the last time I was here with Wilbert getting a dead hand for Ivan. It seems strange to think that that was such a happy time, but it was. I was with my Best Brother.

Uncle Aarno says, Meet me at the boat at supper-time and then he disappears in the press of fisher-men.

I just stand there. I can't make my own two feet

move. I know I should go see Mamma at the cannery, but I can't bear to see her working there knowing it's my fault.

May! a voice calls.

And there's Berle across the crowd. He fights his way over to me and I've never been so happy to see his droopy eye.

What are you doing here? I ask him.

Delivering laundry, he says, holding out a bag. Mamma's taking in washing.

But I thought your daddy got a job at the cranberry bogs?

He shakes his head. No jobs to be had. We're staying with my grandmother here in Astoria and Daddy's trying to get work on boats when he can.

Oh.

How's Nasel? he asks.

The same, I say.

I miss the schoolhouse, Berle says.

I thought you didn't like learning? I ask.

I don't, he says, and smiles his lopsided grin. But I liked everything else.

The cannery where Mamma works is a few doors down from the one where Otto's mother works. But I when I reach it, I just stand there, frozen. I can't bring myself to open the door and see my tidy mother who doesn't allow a spider to leave a web in a corner standing up to her ankles in fish guts.

Finally, I force myself to walk in. Tears start leaking down my cheeks the moment I see Mamma.

Mamma just smiles at me and says, Now what are those tears for?

It's my fault you're here! I say.

It's not your fault, she says, and gives a wry look. Besides, it's not so bad. Birthing babies is a lot messier than this.

A whistle sounds and Mamma says, Come on. It's my lunch break.

We sit on the back porch and I look at her. She seems almost comfortable here with Chinamen milling around her, smoking cigarettes.

Has it been hard for you to live in such a Wicked Place? I ask her.

It's not as Wicked as I thought, Mamma says. It's just Different.

But what about the bawdy houses and saloons? I ask.

Well, it is a *little* wicked, she amends. Everybody's got to make a living, I suppose.

Then Mamma brightens. Here comes my lunch now, she says.

And there is Otto coming down the alley balancing on his shoulders a contraption that's holding tin lunch pails.

Hello Otto, Mamma says in English.

You know my friend Otto? I gasp.

He delivers the best soup in town, Mamma says to me with a smile.

Otto winks at me. I've been keeping an eye on her for you.

Thanks, I say.

Mamma has to return to work, so Otto and me head over to Mariah's Tavern. Mariah groans when she sees me.

I hope you don't need another hand, Mariah says, flipping her braid over her shoulder. Because I am fresh out.

How about a fritter instead? I ask.

That I can do, she says.

We sit in Mariah's warm kitchen and eat the fresh fritters. I tell Otto what happened with Mr. Yerrington.

He sounded like a bad man, Otto says.

But how did you know? I ask Otto. Are there a lot of bad men in China?

You don't have to go to China to find bad men, Otto says. There are plenty right here in Astoria.

And one or two of them are missing a hand, Mariah says with a knowing look.

*   *   *

The sun is starting to sink and it's time to go back to Uncle Aarno's boat. Otto walks with me. We're going down a busy street to the docks when I see him.

He's walking straight toward us and he looks thinner than the last time I saw him. There's a packet of letters in his hand and I don't need to read them to know what they say. He walks right by me, like I am not even there, like I am a ghost. My father passes so close that for a moment I can smell his tobacco.

Now I know why the ghosts howl and haunt the tidelands. It's not because they want to scare you or steal your soul.

They just want to be Seen.

CHAPTER FIFTEEN

Hukkareissu

It's a cold wet day when Kaarlo shows up at Uncle Aarno's front door. His face looks gray.

You have to come home now, he says, his voice tired.

My heart leaps. Pappa's not angry at me any-more?

His mouth twists and he says, Pappa's not there.

And all I can think of is poor Mr. Petersen.

He Killed Himself? I whisper.

Kaarlo says, No, May Amelia. He took a job at the logging camp, full-time. Pappa doesn't even know

I'm here. He and Isaiah and Alvin and Wilbert are all working up there now.

Wilbert? I ask, surprised.

They hired him on as whistle punk. Gave everyone room and board. It makes sense, less mouths to feed.

Oh, I say.

Then Kaarlo runs a frustrated hand through his dirty hair, and asks, Will you come?

I nod.

Uncle Aarno helps me pack and then carries my bag to the porch. Kaarlo is waiting at the bottom of the steps, pacing back and forth like an angry cougar. I hesitate. Suddenly, I'm not so sure about leaving this quiet house and my kind uncle.

You're always welcome here, May Amelia, Uncle Aarno says.

Thank you, I say, and hug him hard.

He leans down and whispers in my ear. You're a good girl. Don't forget it.

I won't, I whisper back.

I'll be by in a few days to check in on you, he says, straightening. And be sure to take your cat.

I don't think Buttons will like being in a boat, I say.

Better in the boat, than in the water, he says, laughing.

Kaarlo rows down the Nasel toward home, and I can't believe how much I have missed everything. I've missed the boys and the fighting and I have even missed the sharp stink of our farm, the manure-mud-mossy-wet smell that is Home. When we near the bend by our house, I can barely contain my own self. But Kaarlo keeps right on rowing past it, past the Petersen farm even.

Where are we going? I ask.

He narrows his eyes at me. The new owner put us out, May Amelia. We're renting Uncle Niihlo's place.

Bosie meets us before we even reach the house.

Hiya, Bosie, I say, and we go into Uncle Niihlo's place. I look around.

The only furniture from our house that's in it is the kitchen table and two beds shoved together side by side. Filthy dishes are stacked in a bucket, and every corner is thick with spiderwebs. The fire's burned out and it smells like unwashed boys. It's cold and damp, and I have never seen a sorrier place in my life.

Where's the rest of the furniture? I ask.

Bank took it, Kaarlo says.

All at once I miss the warmth of Uncle Aarno's house. And my bed. And Uncle Aarno.

The door opens and Lonny runs in and flings himself at me. May! You're Back!

I give him a squeeze.

What do you think of the new place? he asks.

And there's no point in lying.

It's Terrible, I say.

It sure is! Lonny agrees.

The door opens again and this time Wendell comes in, followed by Ivan. But I can't bring myself to greet them like Lonny. We stand and stare at each other like we're strangers and not relations.

I told Kaarlo to fetch you, Wendell says loudly. I told him we needed you.

But my heart is as cool as the shack. I can't forget the last time I saw them.

You needed a cook? I challenge.

Nope, Ivan says, and holds up his stump. There's a wooden spoon tied to it. I've been doing all the cooking around here.

He's not half bad actually, Kaarlo says in a grudging voice.

Haven't burned anything yet, Ivan adds.

Then why? I ask.

Because you're like a flea, Wendell explains loudly.

A flea?

You're annoying, Kaarlo says with a slight smile, but it wouldn't be home without You.

The bank took most of our furniture and tools and equipment.

They didn't get my hand, Ivan informs me.

Good thing, I say, but I don't ask where he's put it.

But there is one other thing besides Ivan's hand the bank did not get and only because Kaarlo is so clever: our chickens. He hid them away in a little henhouse he built deep in the woods.

I don't know how long they'll last with the cougars, but somebody had to do some thinking around here, he says.

Uncle Niihlo hasn't cleared any of the land around the cabin. The boys must cut down the trees and dig up the stumps, so that we can farm when next summer comes. Everybody has a different job. Ivan and Wendell spend their days chopping down trees, and Lonny and me clean the house and do the washing. Ivan does the cooking. He ties a wooden spoon to his stump to stir things. Even Buttons does her part by keeping down the mice.

Uncle Aarno brings coffee and sugar and flour, but no letters from my brother Matti. Now I know how Pappa felt when he sent all those letters to the president and other Important men he was so sure would help him.

Wild Cat Clark comes by and gives me twenty-five dollars.

What's this for? I ask, and he says in a gruff voice,
I caught that cougar on your farm. That's your half.

It's not our farm anymore, I tell him.

It was your cougar, he says.

After we are situated better, Kaarlo says that me and
Lonny must return to the schoolhouse. Mr. Trebble
doesn't look very happy to see us. I think our teacher
would have been better off having babies, because he
has no patience for teaching children.

It's a cold damp day and we are huddling at our
desks doing spelling in wet clothes.

Who can spell Befuddled? he asks.

No one raises their hand.

Mr. Trebble looks right at Charles. Do you know
how to spell Befuddled, Charles?

Charles's face darkens, and he says, *Ei.*

Mr. Trebble walks over and smacks Charles's
hand once with the ruler.

English! he orders.

Later, Mr. Trebble goes to the outhouse. Charles
leaps up and dashes to our teacher's desk and grabs
up the hated ruler. Then he walks over to the pot-
belly stove, opens the door, and tosses it inside.

He won't be able to find it now, Charles says, and
all the children cheer.

You sure got *sisu*, Charles, I say in admiration.

When Mr. Trebble returns and notices the ruler missing, he scowls.

Who took my ruler? he demands.

Not one child answers.

I want the Guilty Party to go up to the board and sign their name, he orders.

No one stands up.

Now! he hollers, and smacks his desk, and across the room Charles flinches. Mr. Trebble narrows his eyes.

Before he can say a word I just leap up and walk to the board and sign my name, my handwriting neat and tidy.

May Amelia Jackson

Mr. Trebble smiles in satisfaction and he looks just like Nuutti after he got in a good punch. But his satisfaction turns to confusion a moment later when another child walks up and signs his name, and then another, and another, until every last child in the schoolhouse has signed his name.

Mr. Trebble's face reddens in fury. Then he gathers his coat and his books and storms out of the schoolhouse, muttering, I cannot teach such Ignorant Children.

We all look around at each other.

Charles grins at me.

No, he says, *You* got *sisu*, May Amelia.

I tell the boys at supper what happened at the school-house, but no one finds it as funny as me and Lonny. Kaarlo is glum and he picks at his food.

There're too many stumps to clear, Wendell says. We need dynamite.

And flour, Ivan adds.

Kaarlo looks weary.

I'll go to the bank tomorrow to see if they'll give us a loan to buy supplies, he says finally.

Then he says, Pappa was at the farm again last night.

What? I ask.

The sheriff came by to see me today, Kaarlo says. Says Pappa got drunk and went down there and scared to death the new owners. Shouted that it was his farm. They're a nice enough couple, too. The sheriff says if Pappa does it again, he's gonna have to toss him in jail.

I look around the table. Again? I ask. He's done it before?

A few times, Ivan admits.

The next morning Kaarlo makes the trip to Astoria to go to the bank and it's late when he finally returns, but no one is asleep. We are all waiting to hear the news.

Did they give you the money? I ask.

Hukkareissu, he says in a tired voice, which translates into Unsuccessful Trip, but really means a Waste Of Time.

Why? Ivan asks.

The man said the Jackson name is No Good anymore, Kaarlo says.

Everyone is quiet.

And then Lonny says, Maybe you should get a new name.

No eggs for breakfast, Ivan announces the next morning.

Some animal managed to get into the henhouse and all that's left of our best laying hens is feathers. But that's not the end of our bad luck. Kaarlo and the boys work all afternoon trying to chop up a big old stump in the middle of what's going to be a field, but without dynamite it takes forever. They chop and chop and chop and by the end of the day it looks no different than it did in the morning.

Hukkareissu! Kaarlo shouts in frustration, flinging his ax.

Back in the house, Ivan is grumbling.

How can I cook without eggs? he asks.

Fine, fine, I say. I'll scare up some eggs.

I take the rowboat and go to Mr. Clayton's place.

Mrs. Clayton, who I still think of as Miss McEwing, is hanging wash. It is strange to see our teacher doing laundry.

May Amelia! she says.

Can I borrow some eggs? I ask.

Of course, she says. Come inside and have some tea.

The house is cheery and cozy. It's everything Uncle Niihlo's place isn't. Her treasured books are displayed on a shelf and a warm fire is burning brightly. There's a good smell in the room.

Do you like being married? I ask her.

Yes, very much so, she says.

That's a shame, I say. I was hoping it wouldn't work out so you could come back and teach us.

I understand Mr. Trebble quit, she says.

Mr. Trouble, I say. He didn't like girls.

But you're an excellent pupil! she says indignantly. One of the best in the class!

I'm not, I say. Or we wouldn't have lost the farm.

That is the most ridiculous thing I have ever heard, she says.

It's the truth.

She sighs. Your people are very stubborn.

The Finns? I ask.

The Jacksons, she says with a wry smile.

*　　*　　*

Mrs. Clayton gives me a basket of eggs and a pie
that Mr. Clayton made with the last of their apples.
When I walk in, Kaarlo is sitting at the kitchen table,
a dark expression on his face. The other boys are
quiet. Everyone seems to be waiting for something.

Supper ready? I ask, setting my basket down.

Not yet, Ivan says.

Kaarlo slaps a letter on the table.

It's For You, he says, looking at me.

Is it from Matti? I ask.

Don't you mean King Matti? Kaarlo taunts.

I ignore him and rip it open and start reading.

My Little May,

   *I am so sorry to hear of the troubles back home.
I would come, but I don't know what I could do
to change the situation and I just can't leave a
good job with the baby on the way. I'm sure you
understand.*

   *I will try and send a little money every month to
help out. Take care of yourself.*

   Your loving brother,
   Matti

Tears blur my eyes and I wonder if Mariah
has anything besides hands lying around. Because
my brother Matti sure could use a heart. Anger
races through me quicker than fire in a barn. How

could he not come home? He promised!

He coming to rescue us? Kaarlo prods me.

No, I whisper.

'Course he ain't, Kaarlo says scornfully. All he cares about is his new wife and his fancy life in San Francisco!

I bite my lip.

Kaarlo explodes.

Matti's lucky! he shouts. He got out! And we're stuck here, like cows in the mud!

And then he whirls away and covers his eyes with his hands and moans, his whole body shuddering like he is holding back a sob.

Kaarlo? Lonny asks fearfully.

Kaarlo looks up, his eyes hollow.

I don't even blame him for not coming back here, he whispers. I'd do the same thing if I was in his place. I could clear these fields day in and day out and they'll never be ready to make hay in the summer. It's *hukkareissu.*

Ivan and Wendell and Lonny are all staring at Kaarlo with despair in their faces and I feel the same way. We can take him being stubborn and angry and scowling and shouting, but we cannot take his tears because if Kaarlo loses faith—if *Kaarlo* gives up—then there is no hope for the rest of us Jacksons. I don't need a lump of lead to tell me what will happen. I hafta do something fast.

I look around, and my eyes fall on the basket.

I say, Who Wants Pie?

Everyone looks at me.

Ivan looks at me like I have gone crazy. What?

Mrs. Clayton gave me a pie, I say. Let's eat it!

What kind of pie is it? Wendell asks.

Apple, I say.

But we haven't had our supper yet, Lonny says, looking confused. We can't eat our dessert first.

Ivan says, Sure we can!

Why not? agrees Wendell.

What do you think, Kaarlo? I ask in a soft voice, like I'm talking to a baby or a skittish horse. You want some pie?

Kaarlo is staring at the floor. He takes a deep breath and then looks up slowly. His eyes meet mine and he sighs.

I'll take a slice, he says.

We have lost everything—we have no farm, we have no hens, and we have no money. But we have a pie. And for a brief moment, it is enough.

CHAPTER SIXTEEN

The Pearl of Nasel

Not a single person answers the ads. It seems that no one can be lured into teaching us children. I guess educated folks don't want to live in the middle of nowhere where it rains all the time.

It is almost Christmas when Mrs. Clayton agrees to return to the schoolhouse. Her sweet face is the best present we have ever had.

Good morning, children, she says.

Good morning, Miss McEwing, we say.

Mrs. Clayton, she corrects.

You got to be Miss McEwing to us, I say.

Married ladies aren't allowed to teach, Charles tells her.

That's the rules! Lonny exclaims.

Sometimes rules are made to be broken, she says.

And I guess she's right. You have to think Different in a place where bulls attack your schoolhouse and you learn in your underdrawers.

Can we break the Rule About Speaking English? Charles asks in a hopeful voice.

Sinä menet kouluun, our teacher says in perfect Finn.

Uncle Aarno's mate Tuuni comes to see me. His eyes are worried.

I think you should look in on your uncle, he says.

What's wrong? I ask.

He got knocked off the boat two days ago. He was in the water for a while and he seemed okay when I fished him out, but I think he might need to see the doctor. Problem is, *he* thinks he's fine.

Wendell and I go to Uncle Aarno's house. Our uncle is in his yard tanning fishing nets so that they will last longer in the water. His head is bandaged under his cap and his face looks a little gray. It's hard work, even for a healthy man, and he looks like he's been at it all day.

Hiya, Uncle Aarno! I say. I hear you got knocked off the boat.

Boom hit me. Didn't even see it coming, he says.

Maybe you should go to the doctor in Astoria, I say.

Nothing wrong with me, he dismisses. I'm fit as a fiddle. Just got a headache.

Mind if I take a look at your head? Wendell asks. You know, I want to be a doctor.

Don't see why not, Uncle Aarno says, and sits on a stump.

Wendell goes over and takes Uncle Aarno's cap off and touches his skull. His eyes widen in surprise.

I think we need to fetch the doctor, May, Wendell says in a flat voice.

There's nothing wrong with me. It's just a headache, Uncle Aarno insists.

Wendell waves me over and puts my hand on Uncle Aarno's skull and twists gently.

Uncle Aarno's skull *moves* with my hand.

No wonder he's got a headache, I murmur.

Wendell declares it's too dangerous to move Uncle Aarno, so Tuuni fetches the doctor to come to us. When the doctor examines Uncle Aarno's skull, he almost faints.

Good heavens, man! the doctor scolds. It's been broken clear around! Your brains could spill out at any minute! What were you thinking walking around with a loose skull?

Uncle Aarno just chuckles weakly and says, Guess

all my Good Sense must have gotten knocked out.

Wendell stays and takes care of Uncle Aarno. The mail must still be delivered, so I do the sorting and Tuuni sails me up and down the river to make the deliveries.

I hand a letter to Mrs. Paarvala. She opens it and sighs sadly.

What's the matter? I ask her. Bad news?

No news, she says. I can't read it. It's in English.

I'll translate it for you, I offer.

A few days later, Mr. Hasalm, Charles's father, shows up with a letter.

Did I deliver it wrong? I ask.

No, Mr. Hasalm says. I was hoping you would translate it for me.

Me? I ask.

Yes, he says with a smile. Mrs. Paarvala says you're the best translator around here.

Soon folks are showing up at Uncle Aarno's house with letters for me to translate.

Eventually Uncle Aarno takes back his place delivering the mail, but the accident has spooked him. He doesn't want to gillnet anymore and he sells his boat to Tuuni.

Wilbert sends word from the logging camp that he and the rest of the boys need socks bad. I take all the ones that we can spare and make the long cold walk through the thick woods to the camp.

The boys are almost as happy to see me as I am to see them.

Isaiah swears he isn't missing the sheeps and doesn't even seem upset when I tell him that all our hens got eaten. But I reckon that has something to do with a pretty Swedish girl named Birgit who is helping out in the camp kitchen. She's all he can talk about.

All Alvin wants to talk about is Ivan.

How is he? Alvin demands.

He's fine, I say.

A guilty look flashes across his face and he starts talking fast, so fast I barely understand him.

I didn't want to leave him, honest, Alvin says. I worry about him every single second but Pappa said I Had to work, said we Needed the money desperate-like and—

I interrupt him, and say, He's doing all the cooking now.

But how? Alvin asks in shock. How can he do anything? He's only got One Hand!

He's figuring things out, I say.

Maybe it was good that I came here after all, Alvin says in a thoughtful voice.

Maybe it was, I say.

*   *   *

I find my cousin laughing with some of the men.
Jaakko's cheeks are ruddy from the cold and his neck
is bare for every soul to see, but not one of these big
men looks at it twice.

Hiya, May, he says. Come to see the boys?

I brought socks, I say, and hand him a pair.

Thanks, he says.

I look at his neck. You want me to make you a
new scarf?

Jaakko doesn't hesitate.

I don't need one, he says.

Your dad find a wife yet?

He's courting a Chinook lady who lives down the
way.

Jane? I ask in surprise, and he nods.

She'll make a good mamma, I tell him.

If we don't scare her off first, my cousin says,
looking a little worried. Helmi's not so sweet anymore. She's a real terror! Yesterday, she got into the
kitchen and spilled the flour everywhere. Cook's still
mad at her.

Huh, I say, but I hafta admit that I am secretly
pleased.

You know where Wilbert's at? I ask.

Jaakko gestures over his shoulder.

He says, You know, you could make a lot of

money selling socks to the men. I heard the owners talking that they're gonna make fifty thousand dollars when they splash this load of trees!

That's an awful lot of socks, I say.

I find my Best Brother scaling a tree like a little bear cub. He's way up high in the branches.

I thought you were the whistle punk, I shout.

May! Wilbert cries, and he scurries down the tree.

It's only been a little while, but he looks different. He's all ropey now, and he holds his shoulders back as if he knows his place in this world.

You're a sight for sore eyes, he says. What are you doing here?

I brought socks, I say.

The men weren't kidding when they complained about how there's nothing worse than cold feet, he says.

You like it up here? I ask.

It's hard, but I'm learning a lot.

I moved back in with Kaarlo and the boys, I tell him, and Wilbert looks down, ashamed.

The silence between us is like a boat in the Nasel. Wouldn't take much for it to tip over and drown us both.

I'm sorry I didn't go after you that day, he says in a low voice.

And I don't have to ask which day.

Wilbert swallows. It just felt like the whole world was falling apart.

I know, I say.

And that's the end of it. I can't hold a grudge against my Best Brother. After all, he's the Only Wilbert I Got.

It's nearly dark by the time I start back for home. I'm on the edge of the camp when a voice calls my name.

May Amelia.

It's a voice I know so well that I don't even have to look back to see who it is. I can see his whiskery beard already.

May Amelia, my father says again, and I turn around.

Hello, Pappa, I say.

What are you doing here? he asks gruffly. He looks so old to me, like a shoe that's been worn out and has a falling-off sole.

I brought socks for the boys.

He opens his mouth as if he is going to say something, and then I hear a man holler, Jalmer! We Need You Over Here Now! and he closes his eyes and when he opens them there is something in them—*regret*.

I better start back home, I say.

May Amelia, Pappa says, his voice hoarse.

Jalmer! the man shouts.

Bye, Pappa, I say and I turn and walk quickly into the woods.

The whole family comes for Christmas Eve—all the boys, and Mamma, and Pappa, and Uncle Aarno, too. There is a Christmas tree, a bare spruce tree chopped down by Kaarlo this very morning. We wish each other *Hyvää Joulua*, and there are venison pies and the traditional Finnish prune tarts. But it doesn't feel the same in this crammed little cabin. It's not the warm house where we spent so many Christmas Eves.

Uncle Niihlo walks in with Jane and my cousins. Helmi is wearing a pair of overalls.

She looks like you now, Wendell observes.

Uncle Aarno has dressed up as Joulupukki, what the Americans call Saint Nicholas.

Are there any Good Children in this house? he booms, which is what Joulupukki always says.

Helmi runs up and kicks him hard in the shin and he doubles over in pain.

I Guess Not, I say to Wilbert.

Soon the little cabin is filled with my brothers shouting over each other to be heard. I'd forgotten how loud so many boys together could be. Bosie runs around barking. Alvin and Ivan sit next to each other chattering away so fast that no one can understand them. Jane and Mamma linger at the stove, catching on up the goings-on in the valley and which babies have been born.

Mamma looks over at me and smiles. Can you fetch some more wood for the stove, May Amelia?

I go outside to where the sky is clear and cold. There is wood enough stacked next to the house to keep a hundred stoves burning, what with all the trees the boys have been felling to clear the land. And there are more trees still. They seem to go on forever like the fishies swimming in the river. Why my poor brothers will spend their lives chopping down trees to get this farm in order. It's like we are running our very own logging company.

The words echo in my head.

Our very own logging company.

And that's when I know. *Sisu* isn't about scaring bears out of hollowed-out trees. It's keeping going when everything looks hopeless and sad. I may be a Useless Girl, but I have finally found my *sisu*, and I have enough for everyone.

I drop the wood and run inside, slamming the door open. Everyone stops talking.

What's wrong? Wilbert asks in alarm.

Cougar? Ivan asks.

What if we started our own logging company? I burst out.

Start a logging company? Mamma asks, a worried look on her face.

Jaakko told me they're figuring on making fifty thousand dollars splashing the next load! I say.

It's true, Uncle Niihlo agrees.

Why we practically got our own logging crew with all the boys, I point out.

My brothers glance around at each other warily.

No more cows stuck in the mud, Wilbert muses.

Or sheeps, Isaiah says, sounding a little sad.

A frown crosses Kaarlo's face. It takes money to buy equipment. The bank won't give us a loan.

The whole room goes hush-quiet.

But I will, Uncle Aarno says.

Everyone looks at him.

I've got the money from selling the boat, Uncle Aarno says. It's enough to get us started.

Then he looks at my father, and says, It's half your money, too, Jalmer. It always has been.

Pappa doesn't say anything, but Uncle Aarno keeps talking.

We partner three ways. Jalmer and me put up the money and Niihlo puts up the land. All the boys get shares, too. What's everyone say?

For a moment, the only sound is the wind whistling through the cracks in the boards.

And then Wilbert's voice rings loud and clear.

I'm In!

I smile at my Best Brother.

Me, too, Kaarlo says. Not as stinky as a cannery.

Uncle Niihlo shrugs and says, I'd rather break my back for my own family than someone else's.

He looks at Jaakko. What do you say, son?

Sure, my cousin says. Long as May Amelia promises to make socks.

I'll even make you a hat, I assure him.

Ivan declares, I'm in, too!

Alvin looks at his twin in disbelief.

What? Ivan rolls his eyes. I still got one hand! I'm not totally useless.

Alvin grins and says, You can count on me.

What is everybody in on? Wendell demands in frustration. You're all talking too fast. I can't understand you!

We're Starting Our Own Logging Company! Kaarlo says loudly, and then he looks at Mamma and Pappa, and some of the excitement drains out of his voice. Right?

My mother takes a deep breath and says, I won't lie. I don't like the danger. But it sounds as if it could be a financial success. And besides, I miss my family.

She turns to my father who has gone still, like an animal being hunted.

Jalmer? Mamma asks hesitantly.

Pappa looks at me across the table. Then his eyes crinkle and he says softly, I'm with My Daughter.

The room erupts into whoops of laughter, and joy rushes through me, like logs flying out of a splash dam. Everyone's talking at once, and for the first time in forever there is hope in the air, and that's more precious than stock or fortune.

What are we gonna call it? Wilbert asks.

How about Jackson Brothers Logging? Ivan suggests.

Uncle Niihlo makes a face. I'm not a Jackson.

And I ain't a brother! I add.

Kaarlo ruffles my hair. You may not be a boy, but you got more *sisu* than all of us put together.

Then Isaiah says, Do you think we can hire Birgit away from Armstong's?

Sisu Logging hires its first man the day after Christmas—Mr. Holumbo, Berle's daddy. And he gets a free pair of socks as part of his wages.

On New Year's Eve, we melt lead. Isaiah's lead looks like a heart, and Wilbert's like a tree, and mine looks like a round ball. No one can predict if the logging venture will be successful. The future is as gray and cloudy as the sky above us. But we Jacksons have *sisu*.

Wilbert and I go sit on the porch on the first

day of the new year. It's raining, but what else can you expect when you live in the soggiest place in the world?

I hold out my lump of lead.

What do you think it means? I ask my Best Brother.

It means you're finally a pearl, May, Wilbert says.

But I don't want to be a pearl.

Why?

A pearl will just get smashed to dust out here. I'd rather be a Grain Of Sand.

Well, you are Irritating, he says.

And maybe I am.

Author's Note

My great-grandfather, Charles Holm, settled a piece
of land on the Nasel River in 1871. In 1890, he was
approached by a group of men with a proposal for
the creation of a town called Stanley. It was a period
of boomtowns. My great-grandfather invested in
the venture, but it all came to nothing, as it was
a scheme. The company had never been incorpo-
rated. My great-grandfather lost his land and years
of hard work. Others fared far worse. One neighbor went insane. My great-grandfather appealed
to everyone he could think of for help, including
President Grover Cleveland, but to no avail. In a
letter to the Secretary of the Interior, he wrote:

> *I believed these men to be honest at the time and*
> *went into the company, but soon after I found that*
> *they were a gang of robbers.*

It is said that my great-grandfather never recov-
ered from this experience and that he haunted his
land years after he lost it.

Uncle Aarno's head injury was based on an
injury that happened to my grandfather, Wendell

Holm. He was struck by the boom when he was in a boat and fractured his skull so badly that the doctor could move it.

Finally, the story of Jaakko and his family, while grisly, was inspired by a real-life tragedy known infamously in Finland as the "Horrible Kumpula Murders." In 1894, my grandmother's cousin, Jaakko Juntilla, was attacked by a neighbor in Finland on the eve of his family's sailing to America to reunite with their father, who was already there. The murderer killed one of Jaakko's sisters and his mother, but Jaakko and another sister survived the attack and were brought to America by a preacher. The murderer was sentenced to life imprisonment and was sent to Siberia and died there.

My great-grandfather, Charles Holm

Acknowledgments

I would like to thank my aunt, Elizabeth Holm, for encouraging me to write this book. Her meticulous archiving of family lore is the reason the Stanley story remains in our memory.

And many thanks to the kind folks who aided my research, especially Pentti Aro for Finnish translations, Bruce and Diantha Weilepp, and Liisa Penner at the Clatsop County Historical Society.